"What are you doing, Cabe?" Summer demanded breathlessly.

"I'm walking you to your car. I was always taught to escort a lady to her door at the end of an evening. Who knows, I might even give you a good-night kiss in the time-honored tradition."

She wrenched her arm free and whirled to face him. Her eyes were blazing. "You really are the most arrogant, irritating—"

His mouth covered hers in a hard kiss, thoroughly stopping her protests and leaving her faint. His hands held her arms securely as his lips moved seductively over hers. Unable to break away, she tried not to respond but it was impossible. Waves of pleasure swept over her like a strong tidal current, sending shafts of heat along her veins. Her world narrowed to this moment, and a man who tasted like her forbidden dreams. . . .

WHAT ARE *LOVESWEPT* ROMANCES?

They are stories of true romance and touching emotion. We believe those two very important ingredients are constants in our highly sensual and very believable stories in the *LOVESWEPT* line. Our goal is to give you, the reader, stories of consistently high quality that may sometimes make you laugh, sometimes make you cry, but are always fresh and creative and contain many delightful surprises within their pages.

Most romance fans read an enormous number of books. Those they truly love, they keep. Others may be traded with friends and soon forgotten. We hope that each *LOVESWEPT* romance will be a treasure—a "keeper." We will always try to publish

LOVE STORIES YOU'LL NEVER FORGET
BY AUTHORS YOU'LL ALWAYS REMEMBER

The Editors

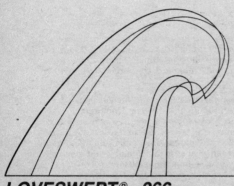

LOVESWEPT® • 266

Patt Bucheister
Flynn's Fate

 BANTAM BOOKS
TORONTO • NEW YORK • LONDON • SYDNEY • AUCKLAND

FLYNN'S FATE
A Bantam Book / July 1988

If you would be interested in receiving protective vinyl
covers for your Loveswept books, please write to this address
for information:

Loveswept
Bantam Books
P.O. Box 985
Hicksville, NY 11802

ISBN 0-553-21909-X

Published simultaneously in the United States and Canada

Bantam Books are published by Bantam Books, a division
of Bantam Doubleday Dell Publishing Group, Inc. Its trademark, consisting of the words "Bantam Books" and the
portrayal of a rooster, is Registered in U.S. Patent and
Trademark Office and in other countries, Marca Registrada.
Bantam Books, 666 Fifth Avenue, New York, New York 10103.

One

Summer Roberts figured she was the only person in Clearview who wasn't turning cartwheels because Cabe Flynn had returned to town.

He was surrounded by the mayor, the entire town council, a number of other mourners, and a gaggle of curious townspeople scratching for a glimpse of the man who had come to pay his respects at the grave of his grandfather, Hadley Flynn.

It was ridiculous, Summer thought with irritation. Cabe Flynn came back once every three years or so, virtually ignored his grandfather the rest of the time, finally graced his hometown with his rare presence, and everyone was falling all over the place like tenpins in a bowling alley. The red-carpet treatment annoyed her, though in all fairness she couldn't blame the local citizens for being curious about him. It wasn't every day they saw a fancy burgundy Jaguar driven by a hometown boy wearing a dark suit that probably cost more than most of them made in a week.

The fine citizens of Clearview, Minnesota, saw

the outward signs of success and were impressed. Summer wasn't. She had seen the sadness in his grandfather's eyes too often when the mail failed to bring a letter or even a postcard, when the phone didn't ring with a call from Chicago from his only grandson, the boy he had raised. The local people saw the trappings of success, but she had learned early in life that outward appearances could be deceiving. To her, what was inside a person was more important than what was worn on his back.

She let her gaze settle on Cabe. He dwarfed the mayor and the mayor's short, stocky wife, who had clamped onto Cabe's arm the minute he arrived at the cemetery. Her attitude was understandable, Summer supposed. Cabe Flynn commanded attention, and it was more than just his appearance. Power emanated from him like an aura. It was obvious he was a man accustomed to authority. There was something about the way he stood, the way he walked, the way he observed the people around him. Against her will, she was aware of him, disturbed by his presence, and annoyed with herself because of it.

She looked away from him, unaware that Cabe Flynn had turned from the mayor's wife and was looking up toward the hill, where she stood alone.

There was something about the unknown woman that forced him to keep his gaze riveted on her. He was oddly curious about her without knowing why. So far she was the most interesting thing he had seen since entering the city limits of Clearview. Her slender figure dressed in black was silhouetted by the blue sky as she stood next to a lone tree on the hill overlooking the gravesite. Her expression was serious and remote under the wide brim of her black hat. The only spot of color to relieve her somber appearance was a single long-stemmed yellow rose held in one hand.

When the service was over, the crowd hovering around Cabe grew as people lined up to offer their sympathy. His expression remained polite as he accepted all the well-meaning statements without allowing his desire to be alone show. He felt like a shark in a goldfish bowl—cramped, restless, and on exhibit. But he understood their curiosity and tried not to be irritated by it. They were his grandfather's friends, and he would be civil if it killed him.

Gradually the mourners trickled away, and he was allowed the privacy to say his farewells to the man who had been the only anchor in his life after his parents had been killed in a car accident. He stared at the casket, and one particular flower on top of the numerous wreaths caught his eye.

It was a single yellow rose.

Jerking his head up, he looked over at the oak tree, but the woman in black was no longer standing there. Quickly glancing around, he searched for her. She was nowhere in sight. Who the hell was she? he wondered with an odd sense of urgency.

She was on her way to Hadley Flynn's house. The stately old dining room was already full of people when Summer entered. The buffet she and the housekeeper had prepared that morning had been set out before she had gone to the cemetery and people were lined up to fill their plates.

Providing for his friends would be the last favor she would be able to do for Hadley.

As she approached the table to check the supply of food, the president of the bank stopped her. Richard Spaulding had been a close friend to Hadley for over twenty years and her banker for nine years. Standing next to him was a large, bald man who towered over everyone else in the room. Even if he weren't so tall, Fausto would have stood out in any crowd. He was dressed in a ringmaster's tall hat and tails, reminiscent of his days as the ringmaster of Hadley's Circus. Now he owned a circus of his own in Florida.

Fausto gave Summer a rather sad smile. "I've often considered the custom of gathering at the house of the deceased to eat and drink an odd way of sending off a friend or relative. Hadley deserved more from people than to have them munching on celery sticks in his dining room."

She could see her own sorrow reflected in the older man's eyes. "You're right, Fausto. Why don't you both come with me?"

She took his and Richard's arms and led them to Hadley's study. As Fausto closed the door behind them, she walked over to the cart where Hadley had kept his Irish whisky. She twisted the cap off one of the bottles, poured several fingers of the potent liquor into three glasses, and handed one of them to each of the men.

"To Hadley Flynn," she said softly as she lifted her glass to clink against theirs.

The banker echoed her toast. "The finest man I've ever known." He smiled. "He was a lousy chess player but a good friend."

Summer coughed because the whisky burned going down her throat, but it also sent a warm glow through her bloodstream. Clearing her throat, she said, "I thought it was you who taught him how to play chess, Richard."

The older man chuckled. "I'm a lousy player too. That's why we were so evenly matched." He took a deep, shuddering breath. "I'm going to miss that old goat."

"He was one of a kind," Fausto said.

Summer heard the emotion in the men's voices and felt her throat tighten. She walked over to the bookshelves built into one entire wall and removed a leather-covered box. "Hadley wanted you to have this," she said to Richard, handing him the box.

He put his glass on Hadley's desk and opened the box to look down at the worn ivory chess pieces inside. A sad smile softened his mouth. "I appreciate the thought, Summer, but his grandson should have this."

"Hadley mentioned he would like you to have it if anything happened to him." Her voice changed, her tone suddenly had a bite in it. "I doubt if his grandson would want it. He probably doesn't even know Hadley played chess."

"I know."

Summer whirled around. Cabe Flynn stood in the doorway staring intently at her. He paused before he came farther into the room, giving her a chance to study him. He had loosened his tie and unbuttoned the top button of his white shirt. His suit jacket was casually held over his shoulder with one finger.

Close up, he was more devastatingly attractive than she remembered. His hair was longer, its rich, sable shade complementing his tanned skin. Dark brown eyes drilled into her, making her extremely conscious of his potent sexuality.

And at the moment that sexuality was directed at her.

Stopping in front of Summer, Cabe was amazed he had found his mystery woman so easily—and in his grandfather's study of all places. She had removed the concealing hat that had covered her raven-dark hair and part of her face. Now he was able to see her eyes and immediately felt he was falling into a bottomless green pool. To his astonishment, he realized her stunning eyes were filled with a marked displeasure. She didn't even try to hide it. It wasn't the reaction he was used to getting from a woman.

He held out his right hand, using the social gesture as an excuse to touch her. "I'm Cabe Flynn. Who are you?"

She looked down at his hand as if it were a foreign object. "If you're looking for the bathroom, Mr. Flynn, it's down the hall on the right, under the stairs."

"I know where the bathroom is," he replied with a mixture of amusement and irritation.

"You must have an exceptional memory."

"It comes and goes," he said dryly. "For instance, I remember asking you who you are, but I don't remember your answer."

"That's because I didn't give you one."

Richard Spaulding cleared his throat nervously. "It's good to see you, Cabe. I hope you'll be staying in town for a while."

Without taking his gaze from the lovely woman in front of him, Cabe said, "I don't know, Richard. It depends on how long it takes to settle my grandfather's affairs."

Summer didn't like the way he was looking at her, as if she were a peculiar specimen he needed to study. She knew she was different from the girls she had seen him with when he'd come to the marina years ago. They had all been blond and gorgeous, with figures that defied gravity and their skimpy bikinis. Compared with them, she was like a drab pebble on a beach full of shiny, bright diamonds.

What was she thinking of? she asked herself. She wasn't in competition with any of Cabe Flynn's women. She wasn't even a contender. She was barely a nodding acquaintance. It was time to remember why she was in Hadley's house and to get on with it.

She turned to the older men. "Excuse me, Richard, Fausto," she said quietly. "I have things to do." Moving around Cabe without looking at him, she left the den.

Cabe watched as the door closed behind her. He was completely bewildered by her coolness toward him and walked over to the cart and poured himself a drink. Turning around, he met Fausto's amused gaze. "Why do I get the impression I am not her favorite person?"

Fausto smiled. "That's just Summer's way. She's like finely grained sandpaper, occasionally rubbing people the wrong way."

"Summer? That's her name?"

"You don't know Summer?" Richard asked, surprised.

"No," Cabe said impatiently. "I don't know her. Why should I?"

"For one thing, she's been in and out of this house since she was a teenager."

"I don't remember ever seeing her before." And he would have remembered a woman like her. "What's her last name?"

"Roberts. Her father ran the marina on the other side of the lake. You used to spend a lot of time there before you left Clearview."

Cabe frowned. "If I remember correctly, the man who ran the marina was usually three sheets to the wind." He thought for a long moment, then said, "Wait a minute. There was a girl who was always hanging around the boats. She was usually covered with grease and wore clothes that would have made Oliver Twist look overdressed. You aren't telling me that girl was the same woman who was just here?"

"I wouldn't be at all surprised," Richard said.

"Summer now runs the marina. Her father was killed in a car accident about nine years ago. Apparently he was drunk and drove off the road. Her mother died when Summer was very young. Summer doesn't remember her, and her father would never talk about his wife. The memories were too painful. That's why he drank, to drown them out." He smiled before continuing. "Summer is an outspoken young woman, as you may have noticed."

"I noticed." Cabe could have provided a few more adjectives to cover his opinion of Summer Roberts, but he refrained from offering them. "How did she become acquainted with my grandfather?"

"She came to the bank when she was about seventeen. It was shortly after her father had died. I'll never forget that day. She wore a calico dress a size too large for her, her face was freshly scrubbed, her hair was as shiny as a raven's wing. It was obvious she was scared silly, but she stood in front of my desk as proud as you please and bluntly asked me to loan her fifty thousand dollars. She was very businesslike, offering to put the land and the boatyard down as collateral. In all my years of banking, I had never dealt with a child-woman like her. I don't know why, but I didn't immediately refuse her request. I told her to come back the following day for my decision."

Cabe stared down at the amber liquid in his glass. "Did you give her the loan?"

"That night I mentioned her to your grandfather, describing the way she had conducted herself during the interview. He immediately said to give her the loan, that he would guarantee it. As you know, he always admired what he called grit and guts." Richard finished off the last of his whisky, then added, "It wasn't necessary for him to guarantee the loan, though. Summer paid every penny of it back."

"That explains how you met her. How did Hadley meet her?"

Richard helped himself to another splash of whisky. "Your grandfather was curious about her, so he went to the marina and asked her to take him out to the island."

"Why?" Cabe asked in astonishment. "Hadley has—" he corrected himself, "had a boat of his own."

"Summer wasn't aware of that at the time. She agreed to take him out. She'd always wanted to see the island, but you know no one was allowed to go there after Hadley closed the amusement park."

Cabe sat down in one of the burgundy leather chairs. He was still finding it difficult to accept that the woman he had just seen was the ragamuffin whose gaze used to follow him around when he went to the marina. Thinking back, he recalled how shy that girl had been, stammering and blushing whenever he happened to bump into her or paid her for the gas she pumped into his boat. The woman who had just given him the coldest shoulder this side of Alaska was certainly not shy. It was obvious she was no longer his biggest fan. He wondered why.

Turning to the giant who was refilling his glass, Cabe asked, "Exactly what kind of relationship did this woman have with my grandfather, Fausto? Just how well did she know him?"

"Not in the way you mean. I've seen them together over the years, and it appeared to me they both filled an empty spot in each other's lives. They were friends, pure and simple."

Cabe was skeptical, but said nothing more. His gaze shifted to Richard, who was running his fingers over the top of a wooden box located on Hadley's desk. "My grandfather told me you were a chess fanatic, Richard, but I don't think this is the right time for a game."

Looking exceedingly uncomfortable, Richard glanced at Cabe. "Summer said Hadley wanted me to have the chess set, but I told her I thought you should have it." He saw Cabe's mouth tighten and attempted to explain. "She only wanted to comfort me by giving me something of Hadley's."

Cabe sprang out of his chair and slammed his glass down on top of the desk. "Where does she get off handing out my grandfather's property? My God, she's dispensing his personal possessions as if they were hers to give away."

"I'm sure Summer didn't mean to be presumptuous," Richard said. "Hadley probably mentioned something about wanting me to have the chess set, and she thought it might cheer me up to know how much he had valued our friendship. As you know, this chess set meant a great deal to your grandfather. We always used it when we played chess."

Cabe's hands curled into fists. He hadn't known the chess set had been particularly special to his grandfather. When he had played chess with his grandfather, he had used the set without giving it much thought. From the moment he'd returned to Clearview, he had been inundated with various revelations about his own grandfather, facts he hadn't been aware of because of his long absences. He felt guilty enough for not coming back to see his grandfather more often, and the constant reminders of how little he knew about Hadley's life were not setting well with him.

In Chicago he was in control. Here he didn't know what in hell had been going on for the last ten years. He didn't need this. The growing restlessness and discontent he had been experiencing lately in Chicago was being compounded by this trip to Clearview.

"Take the chess set, Richard," he said with a hint of resigned weariness in his voice. "Miss Roberts is right. Hadley would want you to have it." Handing the older man the box, he asked, "It is *Miss* Roberts, isn't it?"

"Oh, she's very single. I don't think she would have it any other way." Richard paused, then asked, "Are you sure you want me to have this, Cabe? It's rightfully yours."

"I'm sure," he replied offhandedly, his mind more on Summer Roberts. He considered Richard's odd phrase about her. He was unmarried, but he never thought of himself as being *very* unmarried.

There was an abrupt knock on the door before it was opened. Cabe looked up, surprised that he was hoping to see Summer. But the imposing figure of the mayor's wife stood in the doorway.

"Excuse me, Mr. Flynn. There are several people leaving who wish to offer their condolences to you." The censure in her voice irritated him. He would like to tell the busybody to take a flying leap out one of the second-story windows, but he smiled and nodded as he walked toward her. For his grandfather's sake, he would be polite.

While he moved from one well-meaning group to another, his eyes constantly searched for a slender woman with coal-black hair and flashing green eyes. When he was shaking the mayor's hand and thanking him for coming, he caught a glimpse of Summer disappearing into the kitchen. Since he still had guests, he had to hope she didn't scamper out the back door before he got a chance to talk to her.

She returned to the dining room several times, but she somehow seemed separate from the others hovering about the room. She moved back and forth between the table and the kitchen without becoming involved in any of the conversations. Once he happened to see Allan Freeman stop her by placing a hand on her arm. She gently shook off his hand and continued on toward the kitchen carrying a tray piled high with dishes.

Forty minutes later Cabe escorted Fausto to the front door, promising to keep in touch. Then he shut the door and locked it. Everyone had finally left except for Summer, who had continued to clear off the large table while the last guests departed.

When he opened the kitchen door, she was standing at the sink with her back to him, a dish towel folded in half and tied around her waist. The long sleeves of her dress were rolled up, and he could see her shoes lying on the floor under the table. Soapsuds were practically up to her elbows as she proceeded to wash the staggering stacks of dishes on her left. To the right of the sink and on the table behind her were gleaming plates and platters and glasses, proof of the amount of work she had already done.

"Leave the dishes for a minute," he ordered. "I want to talk to you."

If she was surprised to see him, she hid it well. She glanced at him over her shoulder, then resumed her washing. "It's real odd in this day and age how dishes stay dirty unless someone cleans them, Mr. Flynn."

He leaned his hip against the counter several feet away from her. "Why are *you* doing them?"

"You may have noticed the line of volunteers has been short." Looking at him again, she asked, "Did you plan on grabbing a dish towel yourself?"

Ignoring the question, he asked one of his own. "Why not put them in the dishwasher?"

She gave him a quelling glance. "This kitchen hasn't changed in thirty years, Mr. Flynn. There isn't an automatic dishwasher."

He was intrigued by the flash of fire in her eyes. The dry humor in her voice sent a tingle of awareness along his veins. "Where's the housekeeper? Why isn't she helping you?"

For Pete's sake, Summer thought with disgust. He didn't even remember the name of the woman who had been Hadley's housekeeper for over fifteen years. "Adela's exhausted. She helped me fix all the food last night and this morning. After the funeral, I told her to go to her room to rest."

"Why didn't you hire someone else to help you?"

"Is that how it's done in Chicago?" she asked casually, scrubbing at a stubborn spot on one of the platters. "If you want anything done, you hire someone else to do it for you?"

"You don't think much of me, do you?" he asked idly, crossing his arms over his chest.

"Believe it or not, I haven't thought of you at all," she said coolly.

Cabe had been allotted only a small share of patience the day he was born, and this woman was using it up fast. When he took her arm, she wasn't able to break away from him, as she had with Allan Freeman. He forced her, sudsy hands, apron, indignant green eyes, and all, to sit down in a chair by the table. He pulled out another chair, positioning it with the back toward her. Straddling it, he sat down to face her, his arms resting on the back of the wooden chair.

"Look, Miss Roberts," he said with forced tolerance. "I don't know you and you don't know me, so why am I getting frostbite every time I'm near you? What have I ever done to you?"

She calmly dried her hands on the towel tied

around her waist. "You have the whole town's attention and sympathy, Mr. Flynn," she said. "Why do you need mine?"

She was really pushing her luck, he thought. "I don't need your sympathy. I need a few answers."

Looking him straight in the eye, she said frostily, "All right, Mr. Flynn. I'll give you some answers." She counted on her fingers, as she recited, "No, he didn't suffer. Yes, he mentioned you just before he died. Yes, you were notified when he first became ill. No, he didn't complain because you didn't come to see him after he was taken to the hospital." Her eyes became as hard as ice as she continued in a completely different tone. "Yes, I think you're a self-centered, selfish bastard." She lowered her hands. "Does that answer all your questions?"

He stared at her extraordinary green eyes, momentarily spellbound. She was magnificent when she was angry. A tug of desire tightened his body, surprising him with its suddenness, its strength, temporarily taking his mind off what she was saying.

When he didn't respond, Summer made a sound of disgust and sprang out of her chair. At least by washing the dishes she was accomplishing something. Talking to him was wasting her breath.

Before she had taken two steps, he was after her, his hand gripping her wrist. "Where do you think you're going?"

She tried to pry his fingers away without success. "I'm going to finish the dishes."

"I've never seen a woman so preoccupied with dirty dishes," he said with mock amazement. "You've had your say, Miss Roberts. Now I'll have mine."

He pulled her back to the chair and made her

sit down again. Bracing his hands on the back of her chair on either side of her shoulders, he leaned down, his face only inches from hers.

"First of all, don't answer questions I haven't asked. Second, until you have all the facts, keep your opinions to yourself, sweetheart. I loved my grandfather, Miss Roberts, and I'm going to miss him. You may not believe that, but I frankly don't give a damn if you do or not."

His eyes clouded briefly with pain, then he forced it away. Her scent was floating up to him, filling his senses and his loins with molten heat. He had to put some distance between them before he did something she would regret. He wouldn't regret it, but he knew she would.

He sat back down in his chair. "I don't know what your problem is, lady," he said wearily, "but I'm not in the mood for putting up with it. I've been awake for over thirty-six hours and I've been shaking every hand in Clearview since I arrived. I'm tired and my temper has a short fuse, so I'd really appreciate it if you would come right out and tell me what little burr is aggravating you. Is it me or is it people in general you don't like?"

She glared at him. "What makes you think I don't like people?"

"You stood apart from everyone else at the cemetery, and for the last couple of hours you've been doing an imitation of the hired help. You smiled when someone spoke to you, but you didn't stop to chat. You ignored Allan Freeman as though he were cardboard, which I'm sure didn't do a lot for his ego. In high school he was the heartthrob of every cheerleader. The only people you spoke to for any length of time were Richard and Fausto. I got the impression you don't care to socialize much."

"I had a lot to do, Mr. Flynn," she said, irritated because she sounded defensive. "I didn't have time for a lot of small talk."

"You still haven't answered my question."

"Which was?"

"I'll put it another way. Why am I a self-centered, selfish bastard? There are a number of people in Chicago who have reasons for feeling that way, but I've never met you until today. I admit to being a little curious why you said that."

"All right, Mr. Flynn." She crossed her arms and leaned back in her chair. "I'll tell you why I'm less than thrilled by your presence here. You came back to Clearview too late. Your life in Chicago was much more important to you than that dear old man who loved you. You could have seen your grandfather more often."

His lips tightened as anger and guilt poured through him. Then he took a deep breath and managed to control his temper, even though the guilt remained. What she had said was true, so how could he argue the point? "You're right." Abruptly changing the subject, he asked, "Is there any coffee left?"

He saw a frown of uncertainty crease her forehead and was glad he'd disconcerted her. She walked over to the small coffeepot on the counter near the sink and poured a cup for him. When she handed him the steaming mug, his hand tingled as his fingers brushed hers.

He studied her with narrowed eyes, wondering why that strange jolt of electricity had raced along his arm. He told himself it was only the abrupt change in temperatures that had made him notice the touch of her fingers. They had been cold, and the mug was hot. That was all there was to it.

"Sit down, Summer," he said. His voice held a

hint of irritation, though it was more with himself than with her. "You've been flitting back and
forth between the dining room and the kitchen
for the last couple of hours. Have a cup of coffee
with me and try to stop being such a pain in the
—ah, rump."

Summer couldn't help it. She chuckled as she
poured a cup of coffee for herself and leaned against
the counter. "I'll try to restrain myself, Mr. Flynn.
I'm afraid being a pain in the—ah, rump is what
I do best. When I feel strongly about something, I
say so. It's not a characteristic that sets well with
a lot of people."

"And you feel strongly about my grandfather."

Her smile faded. "Hadley was a very special man.
He had more humanity, more humor, and more
sensitivity than any man I've ever known. Or any
woman for that matter. I would have done anything for him, but all he asked of me toward the
end was to let you know when he was gone and to
open his house to whoever came to his funeral.
The first wire I sent off to you was my idea. I sent
it when he went into the hospital. He didn't know
I'd sent it, which is just as well, since you ignored
it. I thought you should know he had a heart
attack. For all the good it did."

Damn, he cursed silently. He hated being on
the defensive. It didn't happen that often for him
to be comfortable with the feeling. "I was out of
the country when the first wire came. Since you'd
sent it to my home and not my office, it never
reached me. By the time I got back to Chicago,
the second wire telling me he had died was waiting for me."

There was something in his voice that made
her look at him closely, and she saw regret in his
eyes. She didn't want to feel sorry for him. She

didn't want to feel anything for him. "Well, it doesn't matter now, does it?" She set her cup down. "If you'll excuse me, I need to finish cleaning this kitchen. It's been a long day, and I want to go home sometime before midnight."

"Where's home?"

"On the other side of the lake."

Cabe watched her turn back to the sink. She was very vocal about her feelings about his grandfather but she certainly wasn't forthcoming about herself. He was insatiably curious about her and knew it wasn't going to be easy learning anything personal about her.

The dishwater was cold, so Summer drained the sink and refilled it. As she placed a stack of dishes in the soapy water, she heard Cabe's chair scrape across the wooden floor. She expected him to leave the kitchen, but to her amazement he picked up a dish towel and began to dry the dishes she washed.

"What are you doing?" she asked in astonishment.

He gave her an amused look. "You've never seen anyone dry dishes before?"

"I'm just surprised you know which end of a dish towel to use. I don't imagine you dry many dishes in Chicago."

He wiped a plate and set it with the others. "I'm very adaptable."

"That's a handy thing for a spy to be."

He almost dropped a glass. "A spy? Who said I was a spy?"

"Hadley. He said you were involved in industrial espionage."

"And that makes me a spy?"

"You work undercover to find people who steal plans, parts, and money. What else would you call your occupation?"

"Security investigator."

She made a face. "It doesn't sound quite as exciting as 'spy.'"

"Sorry to disappoint you, but what I do is rather routine."

"Sure," she said wryly. "That scar on your shoulder is from a mosquito bite and not a bullet."

Cabe rubbed the same plate over and over as he looked at her carefully. "It sounds like my grandfather told you quite a bit about me. That's not fair. I don't know anything about you except that you run the marina on the north shore."

"Yes, I do."

He waited for her to elaborate, but when she didn't say anything further, he asked, "What's a sharp lady like you doing settling for Clearview?"

She handed him a dripping plate. "Where else would I go? You may have noticed that the lake happens to be rather stationary. It would be real difficult to move my marina to downtown Detroit or the outskirts of Cleveland."

He ignored her sarcasm. That wasn't what he meant, and she knew it, but she had preferred to give him an oblique answer. He had a feeling that if he pushed, she would push right back. He tried a different tack. "This time of the year must be busy for you. I noticed there were a lot of boats on the lake as I drove into town. Does the marina still rent them? I might be interested in taking one out for old time's sake while I'm here. Hadley sold his boat, so I'd have to rent one from you."

She glanced at him. "I didn't think you would be staying in town that long."

He wasn't planning on taking a weekend cruise on a houseboat, he thought irritably. He looked at her with narrowed eyes, wondering if that was her way of finding out how long she was going to have to put up with him. Her unfriendly attitude was really beginning to annoy him.

"I'll be here as long as it takes to clear up my grandfather's affairs. I'm sure I can find time to make use of the lake while I'm here. It's been years since I've taken time off to go sailing."

She shrugged to indicate she didn't particularly care one way or the other. "The marina is open to the public."

Her lack of enthusiasm grated on him, wounding his ego. He tried again. "I'm curious about the changes you've made there. Richard mentioned you've made some improvements."

"Some." The last of the dishes were finally washed, and she drained the sink. "It sounds like you and Richard had quite a little chat. I would just as soon not be the subject of a conversation over a glass of whisky if you don't mind." She wrung out the dishrag, then removed the towel from around her waist. After drying her hands, she hung it over a rack. "I'll be leaving now, Mr. Flynn. Adela prefers to take care of the dishes herself, so leave them on the counter. She always had your grandfather's breakfast ready at seven. I imagine she'll do the same for you. Your grandfather's lawyer will be contacting you tomorrow at ten o'clock. That's in the morning, by the way, so try not to sleep late."

"Thank you, Mother," he said sarcastically. "That takes care of where I'll be at ten. Where will you be?"

She put one hand on her hip and tilted her chin up. "I'll be minding my own business, Mr. Flynn. I suggest you do the same."

"I am. I asked where you will be."

She gave him a forced smile. "I'll be working, Mr. Flynn. Thanks for helping with the dishes. I imagine it will be the highlight of your visit."

"Do you think you could manage to call me Cabe? You called my grandfather by his first name."

Rolling down her sleeves, she replied calmly, "I knew your grandfather, Mr. Flynn. I don't know you."

"I plan to change that while I'm here, Summer. I plan to get to know you very well."

She heard the assurance in his voice and thought he had probably been successful with that particular line before. Not this time. "I doubt that you'll be here that long, Mr. Flynn. Now if you'll excuse me, I have to be going."

"You forgot something, Summer."

She stopped in the doorway and turned around. He was grinning at her. "What did I forget?"

His gaze slid to her feet. "You forgot your shoes."

She looked down. *Oh, damn*, she thought. Feeling foolish, she glanced around until she spotted her black high heels under the table. She quickly slipped them on and again headed for the door. "Thanks," she mumbled.

She'd only taken two steps when she stopped abruptly and whirled around. She nearly knocked into Cabe who'd been following her. "Good Lord!" she exclaimed. "I forgot all about Bailey."

Cabe swiftly sidestepped as she rushed past him, then watched in bewildered fascination as she flung open the back door and whistled. A large bundle of brown and white fur sauntered into the kitchen, and Summer knelt to hug the basset hound. He responded with lapping-tongue affection.

"Poor Bailey," she crooned softly. "Did I forget all about you?"

Cabe realized he had also forgotten about Bailey. For the last eight years or so the dog had been a constant shadow of Hadley's. At first there had been two bassets, one named Barnum, the other Bailey, but Barnum had been hit by a car when he was just a puppy.

What in hell was he going to do about the dog? Taking the animal back to Chicago was out of the question. His apartment was certainly not the place to leave a dog that was used to constant companionship. He was hardly in it himself except to sleep.

Wearily he added one more problem to the growing list of things to deal with. A house, a housekeeper, and now a dog. He mentally tacked on another name—Summer Roberts.

Summer filled Bailey's water dish and scooped dog food into another bowl. Straightening up after giving the dog a final pat on his head, she glanced at Cabe.

"I believe that takes care of everything, Mr. Flynn," she said emphatically as she lightly brushed off her hands. "The dishes are done, the dog is fed, and I found my shoes so I'll—"

"You left out one thing," he interrupted.

"Did I?" She frowned, unable to think of anything else that needed to be done. "What did I forget?"

"What about me?"

She planted her hands on her hips. "You're a big boy now, Mr. Flynn. You've managed to survive in that city for years all by yourself. I'm sure you can muddle through your short visit to little Clearview."

Her slight smile told him she was rather pleased with herself for putting him firmly in his place. She started again toward the front door, but he wasn't going to let her go so easily. He followed her, admiring her graceful walk. Her spine was rigid, her high heels clipping smartly on the polished wood floor. She might as well be wearing a sign that said, "I'm mad as hell," he thought with amusement. With his longer stride he caught up with her as her hand closed over the latch of the door. She opened the door, and he took her arm above the elbow. Whistling softly under his breath, he walked along beside her down the steps.

She sighed a deep, martyred sigh. "Now what are you doing?"

He gave her a look that plainly questioned her intellect. "I'm walking you to your car. Hadley taught me always to escort a lady to her door at the end of an evening. This may not exactly be your front door, but the idea is the same." He chuckled. "Who knows? Maybe I will give you a good-night kiss in the time-honored tradition. I wouldn't like to think I was letting Hadley down."

She wrenched her arm free as she whirled around to face him. Her eyes were blazing with fury. "You really are the most arrogant, irritating—"

His mouth covered hers in a hard kiss, thoroughly shutting her up and taking away her breath. His hands held her arms securely as his lips moved seductively over hers. Unable to break away from him, she tried not to respond. It was alarmingly difficult, though, and not just because he was stronger than she. Waves of pleasure washed over her like a strong tidal current. Her hands clenched into fists as his tongue delved into the moist warmth of her mouth, sending shafts of heat along her veins. Her world narrowed to this moment and a man who tasted like her forbidden dreams.

Finally he lifted his head far enough to look

down at her. Her eyes were wide pools of green, mirroring the desire covering him with a cloak of sensual excitement. He had gotten more than he'd bargained for when he had given in to the impulse to feel her mouth under his. He had planned on one kiss, but one kiss wasn't enough. Not nearly enough.

Gazing into her dazed eyes, he realized he may have found one way to slice through her antagonism. Kissing her into silence. He was going to have to remember that. At the moment his body was demanding he continue what he started, but his mind told him to back off for now. He had given her something to think about. Lord knows, she'd given him something to dwell on as well.

Letting his hand slide down her arm, he took her hand and walked beside her to the only other vehicle besides his own parked in front of the house. There was enough light coming from the house to enable him to read the lettering on the side of the Jeep. Superimposed on the outline of a sailboat the words *Roberts' Marina* were printed in white on a dark background. When they reached the driver's side, he opened the door for her and moved aside to allow her to get in.

After she'd slid behind the wheel, he shut the door and leaned down to speak to her through the open window. His voice was a soft promise. "See you tomorrow, Summer. Drive carefully."

Summer started the engine, automatically put the car into gear, and drove away. Since her hands were shaking, she was surprised she was able to steer, but nothing was going to keep her from getting away from Hadley's house and his grandson. Ten years ago she would have been over the moon if Cabe Flynn had kissed her. Now that he had, she realized she would never have been able to handle a kiss from him then. At twenty-six she was having a major problem dealing with the sensual impact of his mouth on hers. At sixteen she would have melted into a sloppy puddle at his feet, wearing a silly grin on her face.

As she turned onto the shore road, she comforted herself with the thought that he would be gone in a few days, back to the windy city, sophisticated women, and his work. All she had to do was stay out of his way until then.

There was plenty to do at the marina to keep her occupied. There was no way she was ever going to spend another minute alone with Cabe Flynn.

She didn't dare. She enjoyed it entirely too much.

Two

Cabe kept his word about seeing Summer the following day, but not for the reason he had originally intended.

His grandfather's lawyer, Mr. Everett, had arrived at the house at exactly ten o'clock with a bulging briefcase in his hand. Two hours later Cabe was behind the wheel of his car driving along the shore road toward Roberts' Marina.

He was stunned by some of the information the lawyer had given him in his grandfather's study. Cabe had known Hadley owned the house he had lived in and the island, but according to Mr. Everett, Hadley had also owned half the town. Cabe had always known his grandfather was financially comfortable, but he certainly had had no idea his grandfather had owned so much property. No wonder most of the town had been at the funeral, fawning all over him. He now held deeds to a great deal of the property their homes and businesses were built on. Plus the island. That piece of real estate was the reason he was on his way to have a friendly little chat with Summer Roberts.

He couldn't help wondering if Summer had known all along the extent of Hadley's wealth and had taken advantage of that knowledge. Had she been playing his grandfather for a fool in the guise of friendship? How kind had she really been to him? Perhaps it was all very innocent, exactly what Richard and Fausto had said it was. Then again, perhaps it wasn't.

For years Cabe had lived in a shadowy world where everyone was suspected of being guilty until proven innocent. Investigating industrial and business espionage had left him cynical about people and their motives. Because of his experiences, he was automatically suspicious of things that weren't as they should be. And he had to wonder if Summer was everything she appeared to be. She was a different ingredient in the formula he had followed most of his working life.

His hands tightened on the steering wheel. When he had first arrived in Clearview, he had planned to attend his grandfather's funeral, hand over the sale of the house to a real estate agent, then turn around and head back to his own world in Chicago. Now he wasn't sure exactly when he would be able to leave. His grandfather's affairs had gotten very complicated.

So had his life. Ever since he had seen a lovely woman on a hilltop holding a yellow rose in her hand. His body tightened as he remembered how she had felt in his arms last night. He was uneasy with the riot of unfamiliar feelings she was creating deep inside him. Half of him resented the effect she had on him.

The other half wanted her badly.

Coming around a gradual curve in the road, he saw the billboard advertising Roberts' Marina a quarter mile ahead and slowed so he wouldn't miss the turnoff. Turning where the arrow on another colorful sign pointed, he thought at first he must have mistaken the directions. The scene in front of him was nothing like he remembered. Several buildings were familiar, and the dock was in the same location, but that's where the similarities ended. There was no peeling paint or other indication of neglect. The windows in the main building were sparkling in the bright sunlight, the exterior immaculately painted white with dark blue trim. The boathouse roof was no longer sagging but covered with deep blue shingles, its walls a spotless white too. Instead of gravel, the widened driveway and parking areas were all paved. There were several new buildings: a gift shop, a restaurant, and a second boathouse.

He was amazed by the difference between this marina and the one he remembered. Summer obviously ran an organized, successful operation. The whole layout indicated she was ambitious and hardworking. What he needed to know was just how ambitious she was. Enough to use an old man's friendship and money to get what she wanted?

He parked his car near the door marked OFFICE. At the rear of the building he saw the Jeep Summer had driven away from Hadley's house last night. Getting out of his car, he held the door open to allow Bailey to jump down. Then they headed toward the office.

Summer wasn't in the office. At that moment she was in one of the boathouses swearing silently. An inept tourist who didn't know a boat from his big toe had damaged one of her sixteen-foot sailboats. She often wished she could ask for credentials of some kind from the people who rented equipment from the marina. An amazing number of them took boats out onto the lake even though they had to be shown how to raise the sail and steer the rudder. Dozens of tourists rented water skis and a boat to try their hand at skiing, then had to ask one of the marina staff how to start the engine.

Sighing, she surveyed the broken rudder on the *Wren*. All of the boats had names of birds painted on their sterns, a whimsical idea she had put into effect when she had taken over the marina. She frowned as she examined the boat. Her insurance company was going to love this. Her premiums were already high enough to eat a sizable chunk out of her profits.

She turned to the teenage boy who was leaning over the stern of the boat. "I don't suppose the guy who took the boat out thought to bring the rudder back with him after he broke it off?"

"Nope," Toby replied as he straightened up. He was wearing a T-shirt like hers, a navy blue shirt with the Roberts' Marina logo on the front in white. Her staff wore the T-shirts not only to advertise the marina but to make it easier for the tourists to identify the people who worked there.

"I'm surprised the guy even made it back," Toby continued disgustedly. "He said he didn't realize the rudder had broken off. He just knew it wasn't working right. In fact, he chewed me out for giving him a defective boat. He had to be towed in."

"Well, it has to be fixed, Toby. Get together with Jacob so that he can find a replacement. He may have a new rudder in the other boathouse." Curious as to where her head mechanic was, she asked, "Where is Jacob? I haven't seen him this morning."

"He's out testing an engine he's been working on. He should be back soon."

"Do what you can, Toby."

As she left the boathouse, the bright sunlight blinded her. She put her hand up to shade her eyes, wondering vaguely where she had left her sunglasses. She was about to return to the boat-house to look for them when she saw a man head-ing toward her. Shocked, she recognized Cabe and faltered.

He looked so different today, she couldn't help gawking. His casual clothes were a marked con-trast to the elegant suit he had worn yesterday. Faded jeans hugged his slim hips and tapered down his thighs, emphasizing his masculinity in a way that took her breath away. A white knit cotton sweater, the sleeves pushed up to his el-bows, accentuated the height and breadth of his upper body. He looked cool, overpowering, and dangerous to her peace of mind. She had a sense of déjà vu, suddenly transported back to ten years ago when her heart would race at the mere sight of him. But she wasn't an impressionable sixteen-year-old anymore. He was only a man, Hadley's grandson, a visitor who would be gone in a few days.

She groaned inwardly, acknowledging what a stupid thought that was. "Only a man" was like saying a Rolls-Royce was only a car.

Plodding along beside Cabe was Bailey, his long ears flapping up and down. Something fluttered inside Summer at the sight of the dog. That he would take the trouble to bring the basset along with him was totally unexpected, and she won-dered if she should reconsider her opinion of Cabe Flynn. It would have been easier to leave the dog at home, yet Cabe had brought him along.

After a brief hesitation, she changed direction and walked toward him. Stopping several feet away, she placed her hands on her hips and tilted her head up to face him.

"What can I do for you, Mr. Flynn?"

His mouth curved in a smile. "You could stop calling me Mr. Flynn, for one thing."

"What else?"

"I want to talk to you in private."

The change in his tone made her stare at him. He was suddenly serious, all signs of amusement gone. She didn't particularly want to talk to him in private or in public. "If you'd like to rent a boat, there are fishing boats, ski boats, wind-surf skis, and sailboats. Take your pick." She gestured toward the variety of vessels tied up at the dock and on the beach.

His eyes never left her. "I don't want to rent a boat. I want to talk to you."

She studied him for a few seconds before saying, "There's something I need to check on the dock. If you want to come with me, we can talk on the way."

Cabe fell into step beside her. He would have liked more privacy but he was learning with Summer that he had to take what he could get. Without further delay, he said, "Mr. Everett was surprised you weren't there for the reading of the will this morning."

She halted abruptly and jerked her head around. "Why would I be there? I was a friend of your grandfather's, not a relative. Hadley had a lot of friends. I wouldn't think any of his other friends would expect to be there either."

He studied her face. She actually seemed surprised. He wondered if it was faked or real. "Since there was a bequest for you, Mr. Everett thought you should have been there."

She started walking again. "I don't want anything from Hadley. He knew that."

Before Cabe could comment, she bent down to help a young teenage girl who was having difficulty with the straps of a life jacket. Cabe took the opportunity to study Summer. Her white shorts accentuated the long, slender lines of her tanned legs. As she stood, he thought she moved more gracefully than any woman he had ever seen. Her gypsy-black hair was tied back into a ponytail, but several strands hung damply around her face. She looked hot, sweaty, and eminently desirable.

"This time, Michelle," she said, "keep the life jacket on while you're on the boat, or I won't allow you to take a boat out at all."

The girl nodded. "I'll leave it on, Miss Roberts," she said grumpily, "but I hate it. It gets in my way."

"I'm sorry about that, but sailing with a life jacket is better than not sailing at all."

Michelle made a thumbs-up sign. "Gotcha, Miss Roberts. I'll wear it even if Todd Sternbaum never gets to see me in my new bathing suit." Before there were any further restrictions, Michelle hurried away. Over her shoulder, she yelled, "See you at the class tomorrow."

"What class?" Cabe asked.

"I teach a sailing class for ten-to-fifteen-year-olds."

If he had a comment to make about that bit of news, he wasn't given a chance to air it. A woman in a red and white plaid swim suit, its seams strained by her ample figure, stopped directly in front of Summer. She was holding up a pair of water skis and looked like a plump knight aiming a jousting spear.

"Miss Roberts," she complained, "there's something wrong with these skis. Every time I try to get up on them, they sink in the water. You can't expect anyone to ski successfully if you give them improper equipment."

Summer took the complaint in stride, tactfully soothing the woman without implying the problem hadn't been with the skis. "Perhaps you and your husband would like to sign up for one of our instruction classes in water skiing, Mrs. Philpott. Toby and Sheila can show your husband how to manage the boat and can give you advice on how to get up on the skis. There's no extra charge for the lessons."

The woman's eyes lit up. "You mean it was Herbert's fault? I told him he wasn't driving fast enough. Every time he took off in that speedboat, I sank down like a rock."

Cabe couldn't help thinking it would take a supersonic jet to pull the woman up on skis, but he remained silent. It was obvious Summer had experience dealing with this sort of thing.

"I'm not saying it was anyone's fault, Mrs. Philpott," Summer said.

Obviously Mrs. Philpott was a person who heard only what she wanted to hear. "I'll sign Herbert up right away for that class. No wonder I couldn't get up on those darn toothpicks that young man gave me. Herbert was doing it all wrong."

Poor Herbert, Summer thought. The woman was going to blame him rather than herself. "Water skiing isn't as easy as it looks. It's not something that most people can do the first time they try it."

The other woman scoffed. "All those young kids are zipping around all over the lake. As soon as Herbert learns how to drive that boat, I'll be up on those puny boards in no time."

Summer smiled. "Of course you will, Mrs. Philpott."

Mollified, Mrs. Philpott took off to find Herbert. Cabe watched the woman waddle away and asked, "Aren't you carrying the saying about the customer always being right a little far?"

"The customer is the one who pays the bills."

Summer was stopped several more times by people on the dock, and Cabe was becoming impatient. When she finished answering one more question from an employee, he took her arm and stopped her from moving away from him again. Weighing his options, he decided not to insist they go back to her office to talk. The restaurant and gift shop looked as if they were crowded too.

He saw another Roberts' Marina T-shirted teenager coming toward them, an intent expression on the girl's face. Before Summer could be sidetracked, he said forcefully, "Summer, I need to talk to you alone."

"As you can see, I'm a little busy right now. Couldn't this wait until later?"

"No, it can't." He looked around at the various boats tied up to the dock. "Let's take a boat out. We won't be interrupted in the middle of the lake."

Summer studied him carefully. There was no sign of uncontrollable passion in his eyes, so she eliminated that as one of the reasons he might want to be alone with her. It was fairly easy to dispose of that particular motive anyhow, considering the fact that his taste in women didn't include dark-haired owners of marinas. That left his grandfather as the only topic they had in common.

She decided to get this little chat over with. "I can give you ten minutes, Mr. Flynn, but no more than that."

She walked back up the dock, heading toward the boathouse. She didn't look around to see if Cabe was following her, taking it for granted he was. Inside the building, it took a few seconds for their eyes to adjust to the dim light. Bailey had obediently trailed after them and contentedly plopped down on the cement floor.

Summer leaned against a small rowboat that was up on blocks, trying to appear more relaxed and calm than she felt.

"You have the floor, Mr. Flynn."

If she didn't stop calling him Mr. Flynn, he thought, he was going to wring her beautiful neck. Since he needed some answers first, though, that particular pleasure would have to wait. "You knew my grandfather owned the island, didn't you?"

A frown creased her brow. "Of course. And now you own it."

"So do you."

The frown was replaced by a look of disbelief. *"What?"*

Cabe picked up a coiled length of rope and tied a knot in the end. He had to do something with his hands so that he wouldn't give in to the desire to touch her. "One of the fascinating things Mr. Everett told me was that half of the island has been left to me, the other half to you."

She believed him. It was just the thing Hadley would do. *Oh, Hadley,* she thought wearily. *Why did you complicate things?* Hadley had known she loved the island, but he had wanted to be fair to his grandson. After a moment's hesitation, she said, "I wish Hadley hadn't done that."

Cabe tossed the rope back down and walked over to the boat. He leaned against it as well, his thigh rubbing her bare leg. She refused to move, unwilling to let him know his nearness affected her in any way. Her pride wouldn't allow it.

"Of course you didn't know anything about it," he said skeptically.

It took a few seconds for the inflection of his voice to register. "No, I didn't know Hadley had planned to leave me anything. How could I?"

"You know Mr. Everett, don't you?"

"Certainly I know him. He's your grandfather's attorney." She paused, her mind whirling with the implications underlying his words. Exactly what was he suggesting? she wondered. "You are trying very hard to say something, Mr. Flynn. I suggest you come right out and say it."

"Apparently Mr. Everett has contacted several realtors and corporations about some of my grandfather's property. He had some interesting propositions to present to me after he read the will."

"And you think I knew about them too."

He shrugged. "It's possible. There's a buck or two to be made, and I imagine you like a dollar the same as anyone else."

She mentally counted to ten to control her temper, then said tightly, "Aside from the fact that what Mr. Everett has done is highly unethical in that he has taken advantage of privileged information, what you're really saying is you think he also told me about Hadley's decision to leave part of the island to me."

"Well, you may have wanted the whole island, but Hadley wouldn't have thought that was fair to me."

Summer took a few steps away from him before she turned to face him. "Listen to me, Mr. Flynn," she said in a cold voice. "I told Hadley I didn't want anything from him but his friendship. I had nothing to do with his decision about the island." She could see Cabe didn't believe her, and threw up her hands in defeat. "Forget it," she muttered. "I might as well talk to this boat."

She started to leave, but he stopped her with a hand on her arm. "Don't you want to hear what else Mr. Everett had to say about the island?"

She attempted to pull her arm out of his grasp, but he was holding her too tightly. "No," she snapped. "I don't want to hear anything else you have to say."

Applying pressure on her arm, Cabe forced her back to the boat. "Since I don't plan on sticking around Clearview until you get off your high horse, you'll have to talk about it now. Most of the other property I can turn over to a realtor, but Mr. Everett had an offer from a corporation that wants to develop the island. If it were up to me, I would accept it."

He hadn't moved away, and his towering height was intimidating her. Clearing her throat, she said, "I have a better idea. You sell me your half of the island." Good Lord, she thought wildly, where had that come from?

His smile was wry. "I doubt you can match the corporation's offer, Summer."

"Why?"

He gave her a sharp look. "Because they want the island and are willing to pay handsomely for it."

She repeated her question. "Why?"

"What difference does it make?" he asked, suddenly losing his patience. "They're coming up with a more than generous amount."

"And you don't care what their plans are for the island. If they wanted to erect a glorified pigsty, you wouldn't care as long as you get your money to take back to Chicago."

He attempted to explain his reasons, something he didn't do as a rule. "According to Everett, the corporation wants to build condominiums on the island. He had all the facts and figures about how the condos would provide jobs for some of the local people and bring in more tourists, which would benefit the town as a whole. The marina would certainly benefit from the extra business."

She wasn't impressed. "How much are they offering for the island?"

He quoted her a figure that made her eyes widen in shock. There was no way she could come up with even half that amount. Still, she had to try.

"Would you give me a week?"

He stared at her, puzzled. "For what?"

She folded her arms across her chest. "If I can't find the money in a week to pay you half of what the firm offered for the island, I won't be able to come up with it at all."

"Why not just take the money? Why is the island so important to you? There's nothing but a broken-down amusement park on it." Suddenly his eyes narrowed. "Unless you have plans to develop the island yourself?"

He was determined to think of her as a money-grabbing opportunist, she thought, irritated. "Do I get the week or not?"

Before he could answer her, a man stepped into the boathouse. He stopped just inside the doorway when he saw the two of them. Before he could leave, though, Summer called to him.

"Jacob, wait a minute. I need to talk to you."

The man paused as if deciding whether or not to do as she asked. Summer knew she was putting Jacob in an uncomfortable position of meeting a stranger, but she did need to talk to him. "Jacob, this is Cabe Flynn, Hadley's grandson. Cabe, this is Jacob Slater, my chief mechanic."

The only response Jacob made to the introduction was an abrupt nod in Cabe's general direction. Summer knew Jacob's antisocial behavior was caused by shyness rather than rudeness, but not many people understood that. Jacob wore his usual dark green coveralls, amazingly spotless as always, considering he worked with greasy engines all day. He was the only member of her staff who refused to wear the navy blue T-shirt uniform. Since he was the finest mechanic she had ever known, Summer didn't push him in any direction he didn't want to go. Not that it would have done any good. Jacob tended to go his own way, preferring engines to people.

"Did Toby tell you about the broken rudder on the *Wren?*" she asked.

"No."

In a few brief words, she described the condition of the broken rudder. She was not at all surprised when Jacob gave his opinion of the person responsible for the damage, turning the air blue with several choice expletives that would make a seasoned sailor blush. She was used to his colorful turn of phrase, but she knew Cabe wasn't. Sensing he was about to object to Jacob's manner of speech in front of a woman, she quickly asked Jacob if he had an extra rudder so the boat could be fixed without delay.

"I'll take care of it," he mumbled, then turned abruptly and left.

"Does he always talk like that?" Cabe asked, momentarily distracted from their discussion about the island.

"Always." She didn't want to talk about Jacob, but Cabe did.

"Does he work for you?"

"Yes," she answered impatiently. "Could we get back to the subject of the island? You still haven't said whether or not you'll give me a week to meet the offer from that corporation."

Through the open door, Cabe saw a teenager wearing a Roberts' Marina T-shirt looking around the grounds. He had a feeling the boy was searching for Summer. A muscle clenched in his jaw. It was impossible to get five minutes alone with her. "Come out to lunch with me, and we'll talk about the island. There are too many interruptions here."

She shook her head. "I can't."

"You mean you won't."

"I mean I can't. I have too much to do."

It wasn't in him to give up easily. "Then go out with me tonight."

She again refused. "I'm sure you have other things to do instead of wasting your time taking me out. All you have to do is tell me if you'll allow me a week to come up with the money to buy your half of the island, Mr. Flynn."

Her employee was closer. Feeling pressured, Cabe took her arm and pulled her over to one side of the doorway, out of sight of the entrance.

"Say my name," he growled.

She instinctively lifted her hands, pressing them against his chest. "I did say your name."

His fingers tightened on her shoulder. "Use my name and you can have your week."

She knew it was ridiculous, but by calling him Mr. Flynn she was able to maintain a certain distance from him. Though a flimsy barrier of her own making, it was better than none. Still, she needed that week.

Taking a deep breath, she forced herself to look up at him and muttered his first name.

For a long moment, he stared down at her, wondering how his name would sound on her lips under other circumstances. Like when his body covered hers on a dark night in his bed. "You have the week," he said, and his voice was oddly husky.

Her reply was hesitant and unsure. She hadn't expected him to agree so easily. "Thank you," she said, shaken by the desire darkening his eyes.

"What if I said I would like to see you tonight for reasons other than the island?" he asked after a brief pause.

"I would still say no."

"What's wrong with wanting to get to know you better?"

The heat from his hands flowed through her, warming her blood. "I doubt if you'll have much chance to know me or anyone else in Clearview in the short time you'll be in town."

The force with which he hauled her up against his hard body made his intention clear. He smiled down at her as he lowered his head. "Since I don't have much time here, I'll have to take a few short-cuts. Relax," he ordered softly as he felt her tense under his hands. "I'm only going to kiss you."

Summer was no longer concerned with stopping him. As soon as his mouth touched hers, she was more involved with fighting the delicious sensations threatening to swamp her. Her brain told her she was standing on solid ground, but her body felt as though the earth were suddenly weaving and rolling like a turbulent sea.

When his hands slid down her back and he slanted his mouth to force her lips apart, she groaned in protest and reluctant response. Then, gasping, she twisted free.

"Let me go, Cabe."

He rubbed one thumb across her full bottom lip, as his other arm kept her lower body pressed against his thighs and the aroused cradle of his hips. "I didn't expect you, Summer," he said quietly. "I didn't expect to want you so quickly." His forefinger traced a line along her jaw. "What am I going to do about you?"

"You could let me go," she whispered.

Surprisingly, he did so. She was allowed to step away from him, ending up against the inside wall of the boathouse.

"When will you be free tonight?" he asked.

"Cabe . . ." she began, unable to come up with the words to discourage him.

"We need to talk, Summer. It's either now or later."

She heard Toby calling her name. With mixed

feelings, she said, "The marina closes at six, but I have paper work to do after that."

"What time, then?" he persisted, coming closer to her.

She held him off with an outstretched hand. "I have to go." She walked over to the door, then looked back over her shoulder. "I appreciate you giving me the week." She left.

Leaning his shoulder against the doorframe, Cabe enjoyed the sight of her walking away with her distinctive, lithe grace. When her employee reached her, he gestured toward the dock, and Cabe saw Summer nod. Whatever the problem was, she apparently decided to take care of it immediately. His gaze followed her as she walked toward the lake until she was swallowed up by the people crowding the dock.

Pursing his lips, he whistled softly for Bailey to follow him as he walked toward his car. He was satisfied with the few things he had learned about Summer in the last half hour, but she had a few things to learn about him.

Later tonight he would show her.

Three

Summer glanced at her watch after she closed the ledger. Ten o'clock. She placed the accounts book in one of the drawers of her desk and stood up to stretch her cramped muscles. No matter how many times she looked at the figures, they kept telling her the same thing. She didn't stand a chance of coming up with the money to buy Cabe's share of the island unless she borrowed heavily on the property, something she was loath to do. The last loan she had taken out had been to finance the building and stocking of the gift shop, and there was still a considerable amount to pay off. But she didn't really have a choice if she wanted the island to remain the way it was.

Ever since she had taken over the marina, she had weighed every decision carefully, cautious with each dollar. Before getting a loan, she had always figured down to the last penny when she could pay the debt off. Each time she had gone to Richard Spaulding to ask for a loan, there had always been a darn good reason, a sound business judgment made before she even walked into the bank.

Borrowing a large sum of money to purchase half of an island that would never produce any additional income was not a clever investment. But that was what she was going to try to do.

To mortgage the marina further was a decision based on emotion rather than practical business sense, but she couldn't do anything else. The island had always seemed more of a home to her than her small cottage, a place where she could be alone with her dreams and despair, her hopes and fears. The island was her sanctuary, her fantasyland where the future looked less bleak, where the impossible seemed possible. She didn't want to lose such a refuge. Whatever it took, the island was going to remain the way it was. At least she had to try.

She shut off the lamp on her desk, then walked through the outer office to the front door. The security lights attached to the exterior of the buildings cut through the darkness, bouncing off the various buildings and pavements and making some of the property as bright as day. The tourists were elsewhere, nursing their sunburns or taking advantage of the nightlife available in town. The candy bar wrappers and empty soda cans had all been picked up, the boats were secured for the night, and all the equipment was locked away. Even though she had received numerous requests for the marina to be open at night, Summer refused. There were enough accidents during the day when the inept boaters could see where they were going. At night, it was only asking for trouble to allow first-timers out on the lake.

She locked the door behind her and turned toward the lake instead of going in the opposite direction where her cottage was located. She considered going over to Celia's, but she didn't feel like being penned in by four walls. Her friend was always glad to see her, and Summer usually enjoyed Celia's undemanding company, but tonight she wanted to be alone. A strange restlessness was keeping her on edge, an odd fidgety sensation completely alien to any mood she had ever experienced before.

Even though it was late, she knew she wouldn't be able to sleep if she went home. What she needed was to go out on the lake and let the breeze blow away her churning thoughts. There was something soothing about gliding over the silent lake, and there had been many times in the past years when she had needed some peace and quiet after a hectic day. Tonight was perfect for sailing. The air was warm, and she was comfortable in her shorts and the green halter top she'd changed into earlier, after the marina had closed. The sky was clear. The moon gave the dark surface of the lake a luminous shimmer, and she could see clearly across the water. There was enough breeze to fill the sails without having to fight too strong a wind.

She was kneeling on the dock, untying the rope that secured a rowboat to the dock, when a deep voice asked, "Where's your life jacket? You told Michelle she had to wear a life jacket if she was going out on the lake."

Turning her head, she saw a pair of deck shoes below two jean-clad legs. She didn't need to raise her eyes to see who it was. Sitting back on her heels, she looked up. Cabe grinned down at her.

"Now why is it that I'm not surprised to see you?" she asked.

"Maybe you don't surprise easily."

Her gaze slid back down to his deck shoes, then

returned to his face. "It looks as if you came prepared to go out on the lake."

His own gaze roamed over the expense of her
skin exposed by the brief halter top. "It's a perfect
night for sailing. We seem to have the same
thought."

She considered his answer for a moment. "Do
you think you can remember the bow from the
stern?"

"I think I can manage."

"Okay, you untie the bowline. We have to row
the skiff out to my sailboat."

He quickly did as he was instructed, as if he
were afraid she would change her mind. He loosened the bowline as she stepped into the small
rowboat. After he tossed the line into the boat, he
joined her and pushed away from the dock.

"Would you like to tell me where I'm rowing to?"
he asked as he picked up the oars.

She pointed at a sailboat anchored at one of the
buoys. A few minutes later, she climbed aboard
the *Summer Breeze*, her private boat. After the
rowboat was tied to the buoy and Cabe had joined
her, they began to ready the sails, working har-
moniously, as though they had sailed together
many times.

It had been a number of years since Cabe had
been aboard a sailboat, and he was surprised to
discover how automatically he fell into the routine
of crewing a boat. When the wind caught the
mainsail, he held the jib rope, watching Summer
expertly guide the boat through the others anchored offshore. The wind ruffled his hair and
brushed against his skin. Staring up at the dark
sky, he could see the stars sparkling. He realized
it had been too long since he had taken the time
to really look at his surroundings and appreciate

them. The hustle and bustle of the city seemed a lifetime away at the moment, as far away as the bright moon shining overhead.

He looked back at Summer. Her hair was whipping gently around her face. She had freed it from the ponytail she had worn during the day. Loose, it gave her a sultry, exotic look. He itched to feel the silky strands slide through his fingers, and his mind conjured up pictures of how her hair would look spread out over a pillow as she lay under him. She wasn't the type of woman he was usually attracted to, but that didn't seem to make any difference to his body.

There was an inner serenity about her that appealed to him. She was content with herself and the life she had molded for herself. He had known many confident, independent women, but Summer Roberts was different in an elemental way that drew him like a magnet, although he couldn't fathom why.

As they cut through the water, Cabe noticed the outline of land coming closer and closer. Realizing Summer was heading for the island, he looked over at her. The moon was behind her, though, and he couldn't see her face clearly. It seemed he was along for the ride in more ways than one. All he could do was wait and see what she was going to do.

Summer kept a tight grip on the tiller. Originally her plans had been simply to sail back and forth over the lake, but with Cabe with her, she had decided to go to the island. It probably wouldn't make any difference, but she wanted him to see it the way it was now, how much of a shame it would be to change it into a pile of cement apartments. Of course there was a chance he might see it in another way, as a place that had absolutely no possibilities at all and should be sold for the money. She didn't know him well enough to predict what he would think. Now was as good a time as any to find out.

With the ease of experience she steered the boat toward the landing dock. Years ago, when the amusement park was operational, there had been a bridge connecting the island to the mainland. When the city refused to renew Hadley's license so that he could continue to operate the park, he had torn down the wooden span to prevent access by curious teenagers. A NO TRESPASSING sign was posted at the end of the one narrow dock jutting out from the shoreline, but it was to warn others away, not Summer. The old car tires hanging over the dock poles cushioned her boat as she brought it next to the dock. Before she could ask him to, Cabe jumped out with the bowline in his hand.

Between the two of them, it took only a few minutes to lower and secure the mainsail. Summer retrieved a large flashlight from a locker and tested it to make sure the batteries were good. The moon gave off enough of a glow to prevent the night from being totally black, but the extra light would be needed when the path took them through the trees.

Cabe extended his hand to her to help her out of the boat. "Why did you bring me here, Summer?"

"I thought you should see what you want to sell to the highest bidder."

He squinted to try to make out anything past the end of the dock, but he couldn't see farther than five feet away. "Summer, it's dark as a miner's pit. Exactly how am I supposed to see anything?"

She flicked on the flashlight and led the way toward the shore, shining the beam of light ahead of them. "Where's your spirit of adventure, city boy?"

"I must have left it back in Chicago," he muttered. "Wandering around in the dark in the city, all I have to worry about is getting mugged. I don't have to worry about breaking my leg stumbling over hills and dales."

"The last time I looked, there wasn't a single hill and not one dale. Don't worry, I won't let any nasty weeds attack you."

For the next hour Summer took Cabe over most of the island, almost all of which was covered by the amusement park. She purposefully stayed away from a large tarp-covered structure in the center of the park. Their progress was hampered by the need to be careful where they stepped, having only the flashlight and occasionally the moon to light their way. It didn't help that their path was obstructed by overgrown weeds and strange clutter left over from the rides and concession stands. The size of the abandoned amusement park made it impossible for one person to keep up with the ravages of time and nature.

Summer had no difficulty finding her way, since she had spent many hours tramping around every inch of the island. But Cabe didn't have the experience she had. The first time he stumbled over something, she gripped his hand to steady him. His fingers curled around hers after he found his balance and he didn't release her.

When they came up to one of the rides created especially for children, he stopped, looking down at the rusting kiddie cars. He could almost hear the laughter and lively chatter of the children who used to spin around and around in the cars.

"I worked this ride one summer," he said. "I took tickets, hefted children into the cars, and wiped ice cream off faces. I think I was sixteen. It was Hadley's idea. I was supposed to learn the value of a good day's work for a good day's pay."

"Did you?"

"Oh, yes. I learned a lot of things from Hadley. He taught me everything I needed to know so that I could go out on my own. When I left Clearview, I was ready to make a banquet out of a meatless bone if one was thrown my way." Letting go of her hand, he bent down and turned one of the steering wheels. It protested with a shrill creak. Straightening up, he turned to Summer. "Why did Hadley leave all of this here? It wasn't like him just to cast off everything like a pile of rubbish."

Summer leaned against a ticket booth. "I think he always hoped he could start it up again. He never came right out and said it, but I felt he missed the days when he had the circus. We used to come out here and spend the afternoon. While we ate a picnic lunch, Hadley would tell me about the good old days." She looked around, seeing memories instead of the darkness. "It was amazing how he never repeated himself. He must have had a fascinating life."

Cabe paced several steps away, then came back. "Why didn't he keep up the park, then? The way things look now, it would take a lot of money and a lot of repairs before this could be operational again."

"He seemed to lose interest about five years ago. I think he finally accepted that the city officials weren't going to allow him to continue with the amusement park. He refused to sell the land to the city, so it became a standoff."

A flash of lightning followed by a rumbling roll of thunder were the introduction to a few scattered drops of rain. The wind picked up quickly, and the peaceful evening changed abruptly.

Cabe calmly wiped a trickle of water from his cheek. "Any suggestions?" he asked.

She glanced around, looking for someplace to shelter them from the rain. The roof that leaked the least was on the ring-toss booth. Before she could suggest it, though, Cabe had grabbed her hand and started to run toward the one place she had held off showing him. He ducked under the tarp, pulling her after him.

His shin knocked into something hard, and he grunted in protest. "You'd better aim that flashlight in front of me, Summer. I don't feel like battering my kneecaps against whatever in hell is in here."

Knowing she couldn't think of a single reason not to do as he asked, she directed the beam of light in front of him. She heard Cabe's sharp intake of breath as he became able to see where they were.

He stepped up on the circular platform he had bumped into a moment ago and reached out to the wooden horse in front of him. Fascinated, he stroked the basswood rump of an ornately painted horse. "I forgot about the carousel."

Summer looked around, trying to see the carousel through his eyes. The shadowy yellow light of the flashlight didn't present the horses at their best, but there wasn't anything she could do about that.

Moving into the shadows, Cabe approached the next pair of horses. "I remember my grandfather telling me how he had the carousel taken down from a carnival in Iowa and reconstructed here. He brought me out here when the workmen were first putting the horses up. They had some of them going one way, some going the other, and Hadley told them something about inside horses and outside horses being in the wrong places."

Summer stepped up onto the wooden platform.

Her fingers closed over one of the leather reins. "Outside horses were more ornately carved and painted than the inside horses. American carousels turn counterclockwise, so the right sides were the most decorated. If they had been put on to face the other way, the people wouldn't be able to see them at their best." She smiled at Cabe. "Did you know your grandfather met your grandmother on the carousel he had in his circus?"

"It was one of his favorite stories. He had several photos of the carousel he would show at the slightest encouragement."

She heard the gentle amusement in his voice. "Hadley always liked to brag that the carousel where he met your grandmother had been a special antique edition in the Philadelphia style."

"What's so great about that?"

"I asked him once. The Philadelphia style is very elegant and dramatic. This carousel is in the Country Fair style. The horses are carved in simpler designs and are sturdier because they were usually built for traveling circuses. Hand-carved carousels are fairly rare now. Most of the carousels used in amusement parks today are made out of molded plastic."

"I wonder how much these horses are worth?"

"Is money all you think about?" she snapped, annoyed with the mercenary direction his mind was taking.

His smile was slow as he let his gaze roam over her. "No, not everything." Patting the horse next to him, he changed the subject. "Does the carousel still run?"

She shook her head, relieved when he looked away. "There's something wrong with the engine. It hasn't been oiled since Hadley stopped coming out here. I don't know anything about engines."

She shrugged. "It could be the generator. It hasn't been turned on in years."

"What about your mechanic, the silver-tongued Jacob? Couldn't he fix the motor and try the generator?"

She answered reluctantly. "I haven't asked him."

"Why not?" He turned to look at her. "I don't think it's because you don't care about the carousel. You've kept it covered and clean, unlike the other rides and stands."

"Jacob's got enough work to do at the marina."

Cabe could barely see her face, so he moved closer to her. Taking the flashlight out of her hand, he directed the beam about a foot away from her head, close enough so that he could see her features.

"You don't want anyone else here, do you?" he said, revealing more perceptivity than she had given him credit for. "That's why you don't want Jacob to come out to fix the carousel."

She didn't deny it. "That's part of it."

"What's the rest of it?"

"All right," she said irritably. "That's all of it."

"Is that why you don't want to sell the island? You want it all to yourself?"

She had given him all the answers he was going to get. She pushed away the hand that held the flashlight, feeling exposed and vulnerable under his intent gaze. "I have my reasons. What difference does it make to you anyway? You'll get your money one way or the other and then scoot off so that you can continue to make banquets out of meatless bones."

She was right, Cabe thought. That was exactly what he had planned to do. So why wasn't he doing just that?

In the silence that grew between them, he examined her face carefully in an attempt to assess exactly what was going on in that beautiful head of hers. Why it was so important to understand her was beyond him. He just knew the need was there. All of his years of experience in reading people didn't do him much good when he was around her. But then, he hadn't wanted to take any of those people to bed, either. This wasn't a case of discovering whether someone was innocent or guilty. He didn't know what the hell this was.

He should be back at Hadley's, going through the house to prepare it to be sold instead of wandering around on a soggy island in the dark with a woman he hardly knew. She was the type of woman he stayed away from as a rule. The well-dressed ladies with the look of experience and knowledge in their eyes were more his taste. They made no demands on him, never treated him to tearful recriminations when he failed to call them. They knew the score.

He doubted if Summer Roberts even knew the rules.

The rain was falling hard and steady, hitting the canvas overhead like hard pellets. He said, "It doesn't sound like that rain's going to let up for a while." He felt a need for action, any action. Memories were crowding him. The rain was crowding him. Summer was crowding him. Suddenly he lifted her up onto the back of the wooden horse closest to her so that she was sitting sidesaddle.

She automatically grabbed the brass rail to keep her balance. "What are you doing?"

He was putting distance between them, he thought. "I'm going to take a look at the engine and I'll need the flashlight. Unless you want to trip around in the dark, I suggest you stay put."

Since breaking a leg wasn't high on her list of favorite things to do, she stayed put. Bemused, she watched as he wound his way around the inside horses and found the door to the compartment containing the engine. His body blocked most of the light, and she couldn't see what he was doing, but she could hear some tinkering noises.

This was turning into a very strange night, she thought idly. Here she was sitting on a carousel horse as she had many times in the past. Only this time the person she used to fantasize about was only a few feet away. Puttering around with an engine. Somehow this wasn't the stuff her romantic daydreams revolved around. Her mouth twisted in an ironic grimace. If she were one of those sexy blonds he used to have hanging on his arm when he'd been at the marina, he probably wouldn't be as interested in a greasy, broken-down piece of machinery. Instead he would be . . . Well, she decided quickly, it didn't matter what he would be doing with another woman. He certainly wasn't interested in doing anything with her.

The clanging of the tin door closing signaled the end of Cabe's curiosity. The yellow beam was swung toward her, coming closer and closer. Since he was behind the light, she wasn't able to see his face and she felt oddly threatened by his approaching figure. She felt as though he was stalking her. She remained where she was, even though she was tempted to hop down and run out into the rain. Her dreams were safer and less disturbing than the real thing.

He stopped near her. His free hand came up to rest on the saddle only inches from her thigh. There was a streak of grease across the back of his hand.

"It doesn't look too serious," he said.

"What doesn't look too serious?"

"The engine. It just needs a little tender loving care. Would you like to see the carousel working again?"

With the backdrop of the machine-gunlike rain, her voice sounded dreamy as she looked around her. "Sometimes I think how wonderful it would be to see the horses prancing up and down, to hear the organ playing a Strauss waltz, to see bright lights blinking, and to be reaching out for the brass ring." She brought her gaze back to him. "Unfortunately the music and the lights would attract others, and I wouldn't want that to happen."

"Others are interested in grabbing the brass ring too."

"Are they? I haven't seen too many examples of it. Most people want the brass ring handed to them without any effort on their part."

He set the flashlight on the saddle of the horse behind him, aiming the beam so that it shone on her horse. Then he placed both hands on either side of her, effectively penning her between his arms and body. "So you believe in going for the brass ring yourself."

"Or at least trying for it." She tilted her head to one side. "I think you do too, Cabe. Only you went looking for it somewhere else instead of here in Clearview."

"And why did I do that?"

"It would have been too easy. There wouldn't be enough of a challenge for you here."

For a moment he could only stare at her in astonishment. It was as though she had reached down inside him and pulled out a part of himself never exposed to the light. In his work he analyzed other people's motives. He wasn't used to having his own under scrutiny.

For some reason he needed to shake her up the way she had shaken him. He placed his hand on her thigh and moved closer. "It's true I like a challenge. Maybe that's why I'm hanging out with you."

She clutched the pole tighter. Why did his hand seem to be burning her leg? "Don't consider me a challenge, Cabe. I'm not anything to you but the person who owns half this island."

"I'm not so sure," he murmured, more to himself than to her. "You're an unknown quantity. You remind me of those Oriental dolls that open up to reveal another doll and then another doll inside each one."

"How flattering," she said indignantly. "Am I wooden or plastic?"

His fingers tightened on her leg, causing her to gasp. "Are you going to let me finish?"

"Do I have a choice?"

Her spirited retort made him smile. "Since *I* don't seem to have a choice, why should you have one?" He didn't give her an opportunity to reply. "What I meant was you have a number of layers covering you. As soon as one is removed, another one appears. Each layer is more intriguing than the last. It makes me want to uncover more to find out what's underneath."

Uncomfortable with his analysis, she started to slide off the horse. He was in front of her, though, and he wasn't moving. "You're in my way," she said. "The rain is letting up, and we can go."

His hands grasped her waist. Instead of lifting her off the horse as she expected, however, he moved closer. "Not yet."

She tried to push his hands away. "Don't play

any of your big-city macho games with me, Cabe Flynn. I'm not in the mood. If you're bored, go find someone else to play with."

His thumbs began to stroke across her stomach, sending ripples of heat over her skin. "This isn't a game, Summer. I don't know what the hell this is, but it's not a game." He was blocking the light, and moved a little to one side so he could see her face more clearly. What he saw was a cautious withdrawal shadowing her eyes. "Don't slip behind the layer I've just uncovered."

Her hands no longer tried to pry his away. "What have you uncovered? I haven't told you anything."

"Yes, you have. You're a romantic, Summer Roberts."

"Why do you say that?" Her voice held a breathless quality she didn't like.

"You have a fairy-tale island with your very own carousel, your own Disneyland. There's one flaw to your fantasy playland, though."

"What's that?"

"You want it all to yourself."

She tried to sound casual. "What would you suggest? Selling it to the condo people, who would tear down the carousel?"

In a swift motion, he easily lifted her off the horse, then slid her down along his body until her feet touched the platform. "It sounds too crowded that way." His arms slipped around her back, and he pressed her soft breasts into his chest. "I had a few less people in mind. Like you and me."

Now what was he babbling about? Had he changed his mind about selling his half of the island? "I'm not—"

His lips against hers stopped her. "Yes, you are."

The carousel seemed to start spinning as he kissed her insistently. His tongue surged into her mouth, not to taste and savor but to invade. She succumbed instantly. She didn't even think of fighting the pleasure as it assaulted her.

Instead of pushing him away, her hands slid over his shoulders to his back. His muscles felt like corded steel. Strong and unbreakable. His scent engulfed her, his taste fed her hunger. If this was insanity, then she was willing to be crazy—if only for a little while. Her desire was sharp and fierce, greater than anything she had ever felt before and hard to resist when it clamored for more. Now she knew her dreams had been only pale imitations of the real thing.

She almost cried out when he lifted his mouth from hers. He cupped her face between his warm palms, and she closed her eyes briefly to fully savor his touch. Then she slowly opened them again and stared dazedly at him.

Her lips were moist and tempting, her body pliant and desirable, and that didn't make what he had to say any easier. "Summer," he began. "You go to my head like a bottle of Hadley's Irish whisky, but . . ."

The desire in her eyes faded. "But?"

Regretfully he lowered his hands to her waist, holding her securely so that she couldn't run away. He smiled slowly. "But this is neither the time nor the place to finish what we've started. I don't want our first time to be on a damp wooden carousel."

"Our first time for what? If you're thinking what I think you're thinking, you can stop thinking what you're thinking."

He blinked several times as he tried to sort out what she had said. He finally gathered she was saying no. Reaching behind him, he lifted the flashlight off the horse. "There will be a first time,

Summer, and a second." He took her arm and led her off the platform. "It won't happen now, but I promise it will happen."

He was so damn sure of himself, she thought as she ducked under the canvas. Just because she happened to respond a little when he kissed her didn't give him an unwritten invitation to spend the night in her bed. Oh, who was she trying to kid? she asked herself. Him or her? She might as well have the invitation engraved in gold and hand-delivered. The man was experienced with women. He had to know she had not merely tolerated his embrace but had responded with every fiber of her being.

She walked quietly beside him in the drizzling rain as they retraced their steps to the boat. When she stepped over a fallen branch and cautioned him to look out for it, she decided she should take her own advice. She needed to be careful, or she'd stumble into a situation she didn't want. Unless she was eager to make a complete fool of herself, she had better not take the chance of being close to him again.

On the return trip to the marina, Cabe occasionally asked questions about the town and the lake, catching up on some of the changes during the time he'd been away. Summer followed his lead. If he wanted to make polite conversation, it was all right with her. She was certainly more comfortable talking about various improvements around town than discussing the last hour on the island. Whether Cabe had realized that and initiated a safer subject, or whether he was actually interested in talking about Clearview, she didn't care. She just went along.

Once the *Summer Breeze* was anchored and they were back on land, Cabe offered to see her home. She declined and walked him to his car instead.

A minute later, she watched him drive out of the parking lot, frowning in puzzlement. The man was going to make her crazy. When she didn't expect him to kiss her—like on the island—he kissed her. When she expected him to kiss her—like when she said good night—he didn't. As she slowly strolled toward her cottage, she decided to stick to her earlier decision. She was going to stay as far away as she could from Mr. Cabe Flynn. Far, far away.

Four

Over the next couple of days, Summer didn't have to worry about Cabe following up what he had started on the island. There were no more surprise visits to the marina. For all she knew, he could have changed his mind and dashed back to Chicago. Telling herself it was what she wanted, she went about her daily routine at the marina, feeling as though she had been set up at the starting gate, only to have the race canceled.

Whether he was still in Clearview or not, she had a deadline to come up with the money to pay him for his half of the island. When and if she was able to get the money, she would notify him at his Chicago address.

When she wasn't involved with the daily problems that sprang up around the marina, she was in her office wrestling with the account books to ready herself for the meeting with Richard at the bank. No matter how she punched the numbers into the calculator, the figures kept coming out the same. The totals just weren't big enough to support the loan she was going to have to ask for.

She hoped her history of good credit would stand for something.

Her appointment with Richard was on Thursday. For the first time, as she was ushered into his office, she wasn't confident of her financial position. As it turned out, neither was Richard. After he got over his initial surprise about why she was requesting a loan on top of the one she already had with the bank, he bluntly told her she was crazy.

Because she agreed with him, she couldn't take offense at having that particular word thrown at her. "But I need the money to pay Cabe," she explained again. "It's very important to me not to let the island become a lump of concrete condos. If it were up to Cabe, he would accept the offer from the developers. I have to do whatever I can to stop that."

"From a business standpoint," Richard said, "you would be mortgaging the marina and yourself so heavily, it could take the rest of your life to pay it off. I wouldn't be a good friend or a reliable financial adviser if I didn't tell you the hazards of going so deeply into debt." He leaned forward in his chair, resting his arms on the desk. "Think of the day when you may want to sell the marina. I can tell you just off the top of my head, without working up the overall figures, you would be obligated for a long-term commitment. At least a twenty-year loan. The chance of selling the marina and getting enough to pay off your debts would be slim to none."

"I don't plan on ever selling the marina, so that doesn't apply."

"But, Summer," Richard asked carefully, "what if you eventually get married and have children? The marina wouldn't be the most important part of your life then, and you might want to go on to other things."

Even before he finished, Summer was shaking her head. "I have no plans to get married, Richard. Now, later, or ever."

He plainly didn't believe her, but he didn't argue the point. "Then why don't you try to sit down and talk to Cabe about the island? Tell him how much it means to you. I'm sure he'll understand why you don't want to see it become a tourist attraction. He appears to be a sensitive man. Just last night I went over to Hadley's house. Cabe had been going through some of his grandfather's things and had found a few items he thought I might like to have. I could see the process of sorting through Hadley's personal possessions was painful to him. Perhaps if he understood how much the island meant to Hadley, he wouldn't want to sell it to the developer."

"I didn't realize Cabe was still in town."

"I don't think he planned on staying more than a couple of days, but that was before he knew the extent of his grandfather's estate. I really wish you would talk to him, Summer."

"I have," she said tonelessly. "He wants to sell the island to the developers. The money he would get from the sale means more to him than preserving the island. He doesn't feel the same about the place as Hadley did. It's only the money he cares about."

"I'm not so sure of that," Richard said thoughtfully. "When I arrived at the house last night, he was in his grandfather's study surrounded by stacks of papers; business papers, old letters, his grandmother's diaries, piles of yellowed circus posters. He may be more sentimental than you think. He certainly doesn't need the money. Even before Hadley's bequest, Cabe didn't have any financial worries. I suggest you talk to him again. Together you two could come to some sort of agreement about the island if you'd simply sit down and work out what each of you wants."

"I would rather just pay him the money and have complete ownership of the island."

Richard smiled gently. "Maybe it's time for you to think about sharing something with someone, Summer. You've been alone for a long time. I wouldn't like to think of you being by yourself the rest of your life. Nor would Hadley."

Summer tilted her head. "You aren't trying to promote something between Cabe Flynn and me, are you?" she asked casually. "If you are, you're wasting your time. We have nothing in common."

"Neither did Hadley and Myra. He was a gypsy, a traveling man with a circus when he met a fragile, small-town girl who completely bowled him over. The only thing they had in common was a love and devotion for each other that allowed them to work out their differences."

Summer stood up, clasping her bundle of papers and her purse in front of her. "I've seen what love and devotion does to people, Richard. When my mother died, my father had nothing to live for anymore. He drank himself into oblivion to get through each lonely day. Hadley gave up his life in the circus for his bride. He lived to make her happy, and when she died giving birth to Cabe's father, he transferred all his love to the child. As you know, Cabe's father and mother were killed in a car accident and Hadley raised Cabe alone. I saw his face when he talked about his grandson, the loneliness in his eyes. Look at how Cabe repaid him for his years of love and devotion. He practically forgot he existed."

"Hadley understood why Cabe left, Summer. The boy had the same restlessness his father and Hadley had had since they were born. Of course he missed Cabe, but Hadley knew he had to let him

go in order to keep him. It would help you understand Cabe better if you could keep that in mind."

Before she left his office, Richard promised to
look into alternate types of financing for her and
to make a few phone calls to other banks, but she
doubted if he would be successful. If Richard
couldn't be persuaded to give her a loan, it wasn't
likely any other lending institution would.

And as if she didn't have enough to think about,
Richard's words about Cabe kept darting into her
mind at odd moments like an irritating fly buzzing around in her head. There was a possibility
he was telling the truth about Cabe. Perhaps there
had been pride in Hadley's eyes as well as loneliness when he had talked about Cabe and his
accomplishments. Richard had known Hadley well.
There was no reason for him to say what he had
said if he didn't have something to base his opinion on.

That night she sat on the wooden swing on the
front porch of her cottage. The chains creaked
softly every time she pushed her bare foot against
the floor to keep the swing in motion. Shaded by
the overhanging roof, she sat in the shadows with
only muted light coming from the window to one
side of the swing. In front of her, she could see
the moonlight shining on the still surface of the
lake and debated whether or not to go for a swim.
She cancelled the thought as soon as she had it.
The simple act of changing into a bathing suit
and walking down to the lake required more energy than she could muster at the moment. She
wondered if she was coming down with something.

One thing she rarely lacked was energy. In fact
she usually had too much, making it difficult for
her to relax. Even after a long day at the marina,
she would always be able to find something to do
when she arrived home. But tonight all she wanted
to do was sit and rock in the swing.

Some people would call her a workaholic, but to her it was a way of life. As long as she could remember, there had always been work for her to do. As soon as she had come home from school, there would be housework, grocery shopping, cooking. Gradually she had begun to go to the marina to help her father cope with the numerous jobs that never seemed to get done. She had learned to caulk boats, grease engines, and pump gas when other girls were baby-sitting and giggling about boys. As the years passed, her responsibilities had grown as her father's priority shifted from his business to the bottle.

In school she had made one close friend, Celia Standish, who had automatically accepted Summer's situation without making judgments. Celia had the ability to override Summer's attempts to dodge an invitation to go to a movie or to come over to Celia's house after school. Thanks to Celia, Summer had been able to have glimpses of the usual teenage activities she would have missed otherwise.

As the swing gently swayed back and forth, she thought of the hours spent with Celia and with Hadley on the island. Those occasions had been the only times she could remember actually relaxing and playing. Maybe that was why she had been so fond of Hadley initially. Like Celia, he had shown her how to drop her mantle of responsibility for a while and enjoy the little pleasurable things life had to offer.

Her porch she was sitting on faced the lake rather than her long gravel driveway, so she didn't see or hear the car approach. The grass muffled Cabe's footsteps as he walked around the side of the cabin, carrying a brown paper bag. He was drawn by the sound of the squeaking chain holding the swing. He had had trouble finding the cabin. There was no house number to go by and no name on the mailbox perched on a post by the road. If Richard hadn't given him detailed directions, Cabe would never have found her cabin, even though it was near the marina. He got the impression Summer didn't encourage visitors.

He shifted the sack he carried from one hand to the other. As he rounded the corner of the cabin, he saw her in the shadows of the porch. The swing stopped abruptly, and he knew she had seen him, standing in the faint light coming from the window.

"Good evening, Summer."

Summer stared at him, wondering briefly if he were a figment of her imagination. Late-night visitors weren't that common in her life, but Cabe obviously didn't know that or didn't care. She wasn't dressed for receiving midnight callers, especially him, but there was nothing she could do about that. If she got up to go into the cabin to change, he would be able to see . . . a lot.

She said the first thing that came to mind. "Are you lost?"

Cabe strained his eyes to see her better, but she was too deep in the shadows. He got the impression she was as wary as a doe who suddenly spots a stalking mountain lion. "I was lost a few minutes ago. Your cabin is a little hard to find."

"It's late to be wandering around Clearview, isn't it?"

Something in her voice made him curious. He stepped up on the first step of the porch. "Am I interrupting anything?"

"I was going to bed," she blurted out.

"Well," he said casually as he came the rest of the way up the steps. "I would prefer we talked a little first, but if that's what you want, who am I to argue?"

"Ah . . . wait a minute." She eased out of the swing and quickly moved behind it.

The view had been brief and in shadow, but extremely illuminating as far as he was concerned. He strolled slowly and relentlessly toward her, a slight smile curving his mouth. "Summer, correct me if I'm wrong, but are you wearing as little as I think you're wearing?"

Finding a millimeter of dignity, she said defensively, "I wasn't expecting company."

Her evasive reply answered his question. By now he was on the other side of the swing from her and could see that her upper body was covered in a loose oversized Roberts' Marina T-shirt. The fleeting glimpse of her long bare legs when she ducked behind the swing had given him the impression the shirt was all she wore.

He was tempted to go around after her, but he didn't want her to bolt into the cabin. Instead he sat down on the swing with his back to her. Sighing heavily, he stuck his legs out in front of him, crossing one foot over the other at the ankle. He opened the sack on his lap and stuck his hand inside. "I brought some popcorn."

"Popcorn," she repeated.

"I made enough for two."

She knew a hint when she heard one, but she wasn't overly eager to come out from behind the swing. Stalling, she asked, "Where did you find popcorn at eleven o'clock at night?"

"I made it. Adela gave me several dirty looks when I invaded her kitchen, but she ate part of the first batch, so I guess I'm forgiven." He crunched happily on a handful of popcorn before he added, "I put a little garlic in the butter. You should try some."

Summer knew she didn't have a choice. She couldn't very well stay where she was until he left, especially when it didn't look like he was in any hurry to leave. She wasn't about to sit beside him half-dressed, though.

"I'll get us something to drink," she murmured as she stepped around from behind the swing and headed toward the door.

Cabe took full advantage of the light flowing through the open doorway to admire her before she disappeared into the cabin. The tantalizing T-shirt just covered her bottom, leaving the entire length of her shapely legs bare. Her hair was loose and slightly mussed, waving gently onto her shoulders and back. His brief glimpse of her face showed the proud tilt of her chin and the brilliant green fire in her eyes.

Part of him was amused to see how his impromptu visit was throwing her off balance and another part of him was wondering why he was there. He was a man who carefully planned every move he made. But tonight he had wanted company and had immediately thought of Summer. For some inexplicable reason he had felt a need to be with her.

When she returned, he was disappointed to see she had slipped on a pair of jeans. She carried two cans of soda and handed him one as she sat down beside him. He held the sack out to her and she reached in to get a small handful of the fragrant popcorn.

The crickets and frogs serenaded them, and Cabe began to push with his foot to set the swing in motion. Chicago seemed a million miles away, he thought. There were no traffic noises, no jets flying overhead, no loud radios, just peace and quiet, except for the soft sounds of crunching popcorn.

"It feels as though time has stood still," he said, "and I've reverted to my childhood. I spent a lot of time on that lake while I was growing up. I always tried to be one of the first in the water when the ice went out. I used to help put the docks in every spring and take them out in the fall." He turned to look at her. "Do they still put on the fireworks on the lake for the Fourth of July?"

"Yes." She smiled. "They still put the float out in the middle of the lake to shoot off the fireworks, and the boaters still go out to watch the men light the fuses. Last year a sail on one of my boats ended up with a hole in it when one of the rockets misfired."

"One year I helped the men light the fuses. When Hadley found out, I was grounded for a week."

"Every year there's always an incident that makes the city council question whether or not to continue the fireworks, but they're too popular to cancel because of a few mishaps."

Returning his gaze to the lake, Cabe murmured, "It's peaceful now."

Helping herself to more popcorn, Summer chuckled.

Cabe looked over at her. "What's so funny?"

"I've pictured you in a lot of situations, but I never once imagined you making popcorn or sitting in a porch swing staring at the lake."

He paused in the middle of taking a sip of his soda and slowly brought his gaze around to her face. He was oddly pleased she had been thinking about him. "How did you picture me?"

Realizing she had given more away than she should have, Summer made her reply sound as casual as possible. "Hadley said you have a penthouse apartment the size of the Clearview National Bank and that you like to eat in fancy French restaurants. He told me you're always on the go and hardly use your apartment except as a place to change clothes. Do you really have four tuxedoes?"

He had to admire the way she sidestepped his question. "Yes, I do. I didn't realize Hadley had counted the clothes in my closet."

"A man who owns four tuxedoes doesn't sound much like a man who likes popcorn, porch swings, and soft drinks."

His smile was slightly lopsided. "I didn't realize that was the impression Hadley had of my life in Chicago. He only visited me once, and that was four years ago. It was an experience he didn't seem to want to repeat."

"It wasn't because he didn't want to come. He wasn't up to making the trip. Shortly after he returned home, he had his first heart attack."

Cabe pushed himself up out of the swing and took several steps away to stand near the railing. He stared out at the night as if looking for the answers to all his questions. "Why didn't he tell me, Summer? Why didn't he let me know he was ill?"

"I suppose he didn't want you to worry."

His hands gripped the wooden railing. "You were right the first night I met you. I should have spent more time with him." Turning around, he leaned against the railing and looked at her. "I've spent the last couple of days going through his belongings and I found every letter, every note, every card I ever sent to him." Sounding thoroughly disgusted with himself, he added, "Not that there were that many."

Remembering what Richard had told her earlier, she reversed her previous stand on his treatment of his grandfather. To her further amazement, she found she wanted to ease his guilt. "He was very proud of you and everything you've accomplished, Cabe. He wasn't the type of man who would want to hamper your life in any way."

"I had no idea he kept so much stuff over the years. I started out in the study and I'm still in there. He's hung on to scrapbooks, posters from his circus days, newspaper clippings. Did you know he kept every scrap of my schoolwork, every photo of me and my father, even those tacky handicrafts I made in camp?"

She smiled and nodded. "I know. He liked to bring out his 'treasures,' as he called them." In a teasing tone, she added, "I liked the clay ashtray you made."

"It was supposed to be a coffee cup, but it didn't come out right." He crossed his arms and looked at her long and hard. "Summer," he said at last, "I have a favor to ask of you."

"What kind of favor?" she asked warily.

"I'd like you to help me finish going through the house. I haven't even made a dent in sorting out what to keep or what to sell. I'm having a hard time deciding what to do with most of the things I've found. You're familiar with the house and Hadley's belongings, probably more than I am."

"Are you going to sell the house?" she asked.

That was a good question, Cabe thought. It was what he had planned to do when he first arrived in Clearview, but now he wasn't so sure. There were more memories in that house than he had expected. He pushed away from the railing and walked back toward her. "I don't know. I haven't decided. Are you willing to help me or not?"

If he was having trouble deciding what to do, it was nothing compared with her problem deciding whether to do as he asked. "I'll have to think about it."

"While you're thinking about it, walk me to my car."

He took her hand and pulled her to her feet without giving her a chance to refuse. Instead of moving toward the steps as she expected, though, he slowly eased her body against his.

"I would really like you to help me, Summer." Lowering his head, he brushed his lips over her cheek and teased her lips. Then he raised his head enough to see her face.

"Whenever you say, for however long you can manage away from the marina." He touched her mouth again with his, this time a little longer. "I really need you—your help."

Her hands were splayed against his chest, but she wasn't pushing him away. "When I said I'd have to think about it, I didn't mean only two minutes. I'd like a little more time."

"I don't have a lot of time. I called my office today. An investigation I've been working on could require me to leave any day. A friend of mine could lose his business, and I promised to help find out who was stealing secret plans from his company."

He was asking her to speed up his return to Chicago, she thought. There had to be something funny about that, but she didn't feel like laughing. "You're more like Hadley than I thought. He wouldn't accept what he called shilly-shallying either."

"It will be easier if you just agree now, Summer. I can be very persuasive if I set my mind to it."

He moved his hands gently over her shoulders, feeling the finely sculptured bones beneath the flesh and cloth. It was obvious she wore nothing under the T-shirt, and he was more than tempted to cup the rich fullness of her breasts in his palms. That time would come. It was a promise he made to himself.

His gaze centered on her mouth. "Hadley was a master at the bulldozer technique. It works better than the water-on-a-stone method of wearing down an opponent." His hand caressed her cheek, his thumb stroking across her bottom lip. "Do it for Hadley, if not for me."

She sighed heavily. Her warm breath grazed his thumb, and he was startled by a strong surge of desire. "All right, Cabe. I can't promise I can give you much time, but I'll do what I can."

Relief flowed through him. Not only because he would finish going through Hadley's house more quickly, but because he could spend more time with her. He took her arm again and drew her toward the steps. When he happened to look down, he noticed she didn't have any shoes on.

"Maybe walking to my car isn't such a good idea. The gravel will be hard on your feet."

She continued down the steps. "Don't worry about it. I've been going barefooted most of my life." Glancing up at him, she grinned. "We can't break Hadley's rule about escorting a guest to his car, now can we?"

He smiled, and his fingers tightened around her arm. "Part of Hadley's instructions about the end of a date was a good-night kiss."

Walking a little faster, Summer stared straight ahead. "I'm not a purist. Neither was Hadley. And this isn't the end of a date. I'm sure he would approve of variations on the theme."

They reached Cabe's car, and he slid his hand into the pocket of his jeans for his keys. "I hope you aren't thinking of giving me a chaste handshake or a pat on the head, like you gave Bailey," he said as he opened his door.

She kept the door between them, placing her hand on the top of it. "I was thinking of a gentle wave of the hand as you drive off," she said lightly.

He drew one of his keys across the back of her hand. "Think again. We've gone past the polite-gesture stage."

He held the key in more ways than one, she thought, marveling at how the cold metal could radiate such heat from his hand to hers. "Since you've had the benefit of Hadley's words of wisdom more than I have, I suggest I leave the choice up to you."

He lifted the key from her hand, replacing it with his own. "If the choice was left up to me, I wouldn't leave at all, Summer. Not until morning."

The serious tone of his voice was mirrored by the dark, sensual promise in his eyes. Her heart raced, her breath stopped. She slid her hand from under his and gave him a faint smile as she backed away several steps. "I think I'll make the choice after all. Good night, Cabe."

He knew he could change her mind. Oddly enough, even though he wanted her badly, he didn't take advantage of the physical attraction between them to pressure her into something she wasn't ready for. He would wait until she wanted him fully and naturally, without reservation. As long as he didn't have to wait too long.

A corner of his mouth lifted gently. "Good night, Summer."

She watched him back out of the driveway and wondered why he had come in the first place. To get her help to clear up Hadley's house was an obvious reason, but she had the feeling that wasn't the one. She would like to think he had simply wanted her company, but she was more realistic than that. Perhaps he had just wanted anyone's company and she was the only person he knew in town.

Walking slowly back to her cottage, she couldn't help feeling apprehensive about going to Hadley's house while Cabe was there. Such proximity to him could bring her dreams into reality, which could turn out to be painful. Her dreams were safe, her fantasies were her own, affecting no one but herself. Years ago when Cabe had come to the marina, she had watched him in fascination from a distance. Once she had become friends with Hadley, she had never gone to his house when his grandson was visiting. The old man's eyes had been too sharp, his perceptions too keen, not to notice how she was feeling, and she hadn't wanted that.

She had learned why her adolescent yearning for Cabe was called a crush. He had had the power to crush her finest feelings when his glance would slide past her as though she didn't exist. The lesson she had learned early was not to want something she couldn't have.

And she couldn't have Cabe Flynn.

On the porch, she sat down on the swing again and picked up the sack of popcorn. Idly munching on several kernels, she thought of the time Hadley had told her to reach out and grab the brass ring every opportunity she got. Should she grab at the chance to spend some time with Cabe? Few people have an opportunity to make their fleeting dreams come true, she told herself. She might end up having regrets, but she would also have some memories. All she had now was the present, an empty stretch of days during which she catered to the needs of anonymous tourists, here today and gone tomorrow.

Maybe it was time to consider her own needs as a woman.

Five

The following day started out as a typical Friday. A large number of tourists had arrived to start their weekend early at the lake, adding to the boating enthusiasts already there. When Summer returned to the boathouse after teaching a sailing class, she found Jacob grumbling more than usual about the people who flocked around the boats like hungry seagulls.

Since it was his normal complaint, she only smiled and said, "If they didn't take our boats out, we wouldn't have much use for the marina. You and I would be out of a job."

"The boats is one thing," he mumbled, wiping his hands on a rag. "My tools is something else. They better be clean when he brings them back."

"What are you talking about?" she asked.

"That fella borrowed some tools."

Holding onto her patience by a mere thread, she asked, "What fella?"

"That Flynn fella you had here the other day. He marched in here about an hour ago and asked as bold as sin for a wrench, a hammer, and some machine oil." After a few pithy swearwords describing Cabe's ancestors, Jacob said, "He being a friend of yours, I couldn't see how I could stop him from taking what he wanted."

"Did Cabe say why he wanted the tools?"

Jacob shook his head. "He took them with him on the *Starling*."

Summer walked to the open doorway of the boathouse and scanned the lake for the sailboat, but it was impossible to make out that particular boat from all the others cruising around. The lake was five miles wide and nine miles long. He could be anywhere. "Did he say where he was going?"

"Nope. And I didn't ask."

Considering the subject closed, Jacob went back to his work, leaving Summer to get on with hers. She headed toward the office to check the log. Last night Cabe hadn't said anything about renting a boat, and she was puzzled why he had chosen today to go sailing. And with a handful of tools. The rental log could tell her how long he planned to be out in the boat but not why. She would have to wait for him to come back to find that out.

She had a long wait. All the other boats had been returned and she was working in the office when she happened to glance out the window and see him pulling the sailboat up onto the sand alongside the others. The smaller sailboats all had detachable rudders to make it easier to drag the boats out of the water. The two large sailboats were tied to the dock during the day, then moored at a buoy at night. It was just as well Cabe had taken a smaller sailboat, she thought, since all her staff had left for the day and it was difficult for her to tie up the boat alone.

As Cabe secured the sail, she leaned closer to the window. Usually her first concern would be the condition of the boat. But the *Starling* could have been in six pieces and she wouldn't have noticed. She didn't even look at the boat. She was too interested in Cabe's appearance. She grabbed a pair of binoculars off the top of the file cabinet and adjusted them so that she could focus clearly on Cabe.

His faded jeans and navy sweatshirt were smeared liberally with grease, as though he had been under a car all day working on an engine. A black streak across the side of his face matched the grime covering his hands and forearms. Since the sailboat didn't have an engine, he couldn't have gotten so filthy on the boat. Unless he'd started out in those clothes, he had gone somewhere to muck about in grease.

As he began to gather up the tools he had borrowed from Jacob, she lowered the binoculars. He was leaving. She dropped the binoculars onto the top of her desk and quickly locked the middle drawer. Rushing over to the safe, she slammed the heavy door shut and twirled the combination dial. She snapped off the desk lamp, then closed and locked her office door behind her. A quick glance around the reception room assured her the security lights were on and everything was where it should be.

As she locked the outside door, she looked over her shoulder toward the beach. She couldn't see Cabe anywhere. She shifted her gaze to the parking lot, but neither he nor his car were there. Damn. He had gone. He had to have known she was still there, so why had he left without talking to her? What was he trying to hide?

Whatever it was, she was going to find out. She hadn't planned on going to Hadley's tonight, but now she decided she would. She wanted to find out what Cabe had been doing.

Later as she was getting ready, she told herself she wasn't really dressing up for Cabe. It was only that she felt like a change from the shorts and T-shirts she wore every day. The deep purple silk blouse felt soft and sensuous against her skin. She tucked it into white slacks and fastened a belt around her waist. She left her hair down, flowing softly over her shoulders and around her face. Her only jewelry was a pair of gold hoop earrings, a gift from Celia when she had graduated from high school.

Looking critically into the full-length mirror, she could only stare at the sensual woman gazing back at her. It was a woman she rarely saw or allowed anyone else to see. She had purposely tamped down her femininity over the years, and she was a little alarmed to find it emerging now. There had been times in the past when men had approached her, but she had never been tempted to let the butterfly escape the cocoon she had wrapped around herself. Until now. Until Cabe Flynn had come back.

She had to return to the office when she remembered her sandals were still under her desk. She had left them there after changing into deck shoes earlier.

The phone rang while she was fastening one of the straps, and her first thought was it might be Cabe calling her. Then she realized that was ridiculous. He had had all the opportunity in the world to talk to her earlier. There was no reason for him to be phoning her now.

She attempted to put her other sandal on as she leaned forward to answer the phone. She lost her balance and rapped her elbow sharply on the edge of the desk. Instead of "hello," a succulent cuss word escaped her before she could call it back.

"Well, hello to you too. What brought on that cordial greeting?"

Collapsing on the chair, Summer rubbed her injured elbow. "Hi, Celia. I just cracked my elbow. How are you?"

"Still pregnant," Celia said dryly. "Other than that, I'm on top of the world. I'm calling to see if you want to come around tonight. I feel like making a horrible big batch of fudge and I could use some help eating it."

"It sounds like a tempting invitation, Celia, but I can't tonight."

"You're turning down fudge? Are you sick?"

Summer smiled. "I'm fine. It's just that I've made other plans for tonight."

"Don't tell me, let me guess. You're going to polish some brass or check some riggings."

"Believe it or not, I'm going out."

For once, Celia didn't have a quick comeback. "Going out, as in a date with a man?" she asked cautiously.

Summer's mouth twisted. "You don't have to sound so surprised. I have gone out with a man before."

"I can count on one hand the number of dates you've had this year. So who managed to pry you away from work and when can I meet him?"

It was a shame to squelch Celia's joy but she wasn't going to lie to her friend. "It's not exactly a date. I'm going over to Hadley's to help Cabe sort through a few things. You remember Cabe Flynn, don't you?"

"Of course, I remember Cabe. He isn't someone you easily forget. Harry's seen him since he got back. He wanted him to know how sorry we were to miss Hadley's funeral but we were out of town visiting Harry's mother. It was the last time we could make the trip before the baby comes." Celia whistled softly. "So you're seeing Cabe tonight. How interesting."

"Not the way your romantic mind is conjuring up. It's just to help him out."

"Of course," Celia drawled. "And if you don't tell me all about it tomorrow, I'll never forgive you. Why don't you come over for dinner tomorrow night? Apparently we have some catching up to do. I want to hear about you and Cabe Flynn, and you can hear about the fun of being pregnant."

Laughing, Summer agreed. "All right. I'll be there, but you're going to be disappointed. There is no me and Cabe Flynn to talk about."

"Maybe after tonight there will be."

Before Summer could tell her she was wrong, Celia had hung up. Tomorrow night would be soon enough to set the record straight with Celia. Slipping on her other sandal, she pushed the phone conversation out of her mind. For tonight, she had to concentrate on talking to Cabe, or rather, getting some answers from him.

As she drove to Hadley's, she knew she should have phoned first to make sure he was there, but she wanted to leave it up to fate. If he was there, then she would have it out with him about the boat. If he wasn't, she would have to find another time.

When she rang the doorbell, she expected to see Adela. But when the door opened, Cabe stood in front of her. For a moment all she could do was stare at him. She told herself she was only looking for any sign of his earlier activities, but there wasn't a spot of grease on his jeans, his dark green shirt, or his face and hands. When she met his eyes, she had to admit she was looking for more, some reaction to her sudden appearance on his doorstep.

His hands reached out for her. "I was hoping you would come tonight, Summer."

She was pulled against his chest as his mouth closed over hers, taking her breath and giving her life. All too soon, he raised his head and gazed down at her, his hands still holding her securely along his hard body.

His warm gaze flowed over her. He clearly approved of the way she looked, for his smile changed slightly. "Although I liked the T-shirt you wore last night, it's good to see you no matter what you're wearing."

"You didn't seem to think so earlier today."

He frowned, then his expression changed to comprehension. "You saw me at the marina."

She nodded briefly. "When you were bringing the boat in." She lightly touched his shirt. "You've changed your clothes."

Cabe could see she was dying to ask him why he had been so grimy before, but was going the long way around. He smiled slowly. "Yes, I have." He copied her motion of touching his shirt by lifting the soft fabric of her shirt between two fingers. "So have you."

"I didn't change clothes because I had been wallowing around in grease."

"Why don't you just come out and ask me what I've been doing?"

"Would you answer me if I did?"

He shook his head. "Not yet." His fingers trailed up her neck to trace the delicate line of her jaw. "I want to surprise you."

"You've been doing that ever since you arrived in town."

"Give me a few more days and I'll show you what I've been doing."

Suddenly she knew, and was amazed it hadn't occurred to her before. "You went to the island."

Disappointment flickered in his eyes. "I was only on my half of the island."

She heard the amusement in his voice but she didn't think it was funny. "What were you doing there?"

"Don't ruin the surprise." Stepping back from her, he opened the door wider. "Come on in."

She wasn't satisfied with his answer, but she was beginning to learn that Cabe wouldn't be pushed any further than he wanted to go. He was more like Hadley than she'd thought. "Where's Adela?"

"She's visiting her sister for a week." He ushered her into the library without any delay. When she stopped suddenly and gaped, he gave her a twisted smile. "Now you know why I sent Adela away. I thought it would be kinder to keep her out of the house for the time being. She kept giving me dirty looks everytime she walked by this room."

"I can understand why," Summer murmured as she stepped carefully around a wooden trunk, two scrapbooks, and a set of lead soldiers. They were lined up on the floor as though they were about to fight a battle with the small clay ashtray Cabe had made in camp. Bailey was resting under the desk with his head between his paws, completely oblivious to the chaos around him.

The library was like a disaster area, Summer decided. "It doesn't look as though you've packed anything at all."

"I haven't."

"You're going to have to decide what you want to keep and what you want to get rid of, Cabe. I can't do that."

"I have decided."

She sighed heavily, wondering how long it was going to take to make even a dent in the jumble of memorabilia lying around the room. "Where do we start?"

"By putting everything back where it's supposed to be."

She jerked her head around to look at him. "Why?"

Watching her carefully, he said, "I've decided not to sell the house, at least not for a while."

This was getting more and more confusing, she thought. "Wait a minute. Wait just a cotton-pickin' minute," she said heatedly. "Last night you asked me to come here to help you sort out things. Less than twenty-four hours later you plan to keep the house. So tell me, why am I here?"

"I was hoping you were here to see me." He shrugged as if that were just a passing thought. "But if you need a practical reason, you can help me put everything back."

She moved a scrapbook over on the sofa so that she could sit down. Collapsing heavily onto the upholstered cushions, she leaned back and kept her gaze on Cabe. "You're just full of surprises today, aren't you." Her voice sounded both weary and strained.

"It was somewhat of a surprise to me too." He picked up a stack of scrapbooks and placed them on top of a small, worn leather trunk. "There's too much here to simply pack into crates and store somewhere. I'm going to ask Fausto what he wants of all the circus memorabilia. There's also Adela and Bailey. This is their home. Other arrangements would have to be made for them if the house were sold out from under them. It's not something that can be done overnight. Neither one would be happy in my apartment in Chicago."

From his last statement, Summer gathered he didn't plan on staying in the house indefinitely himself, only keeping it intact for the time being until he could find alternate homes for the house-keeper and the dog. She should be pleased he was thinking of the welfare of Hadley's companions, but she couldn't help being disappointed he wasn't keeping the house for his own use.

Quickly squelching her personal feelings, she slipped onto the floor and began putting the lead soldiers back into their wooden box.

"Hadley kept these in the cupboard under the bookshelves," she said, and pointed to the scrapbooks. "Those go on the bottom shelf of the bookcase to the left of the fireplace."

Cabe put them back. "While I was looking through the scrapbooks from these last few years, I discovered that one thing was missing."

"What's that?" she asked without looking up.

"You."

She raised her eyes to meet his. "What about me?"

"Hadley loved taking pictures. There are scrapbooks full of photos of my grandmother, my parents, me, his dogs, Richard, Fausto, various members of his circus family, Adela, everyone who touched his life. I even saw some of the island and the corner drugstore where he used to go to chat with the owner, Bill something or other."

"Krebs."

"There's a box of photographs of all sorts of subjects. There was a picture of a robin's nest built in a bend of the gutter. He snapped everything, from a spiderweb to a dewdrop on a rose petal." He gazed at her intently. "I've looked through every scrapbook here. I haven't found a single picture of you in any of them."

She began gathering old circus programs into a neat stack. "That's because he gave me the scrapbooks with my pictures in them a couple of months before he died. He probably thought no one would want them but me."

He took the programs from her. "How did he do it?"

She watched as he dropped the programs into an open trunk. "Do what? Take the pictures or give me the scrapbooks?"

He walked back to her. Standing over her, he let a finger run smoothly across her cheek. "How did Hadley get to know you? How did he manage to get through that shell you wrap around yourself? Why didn't he ever mention you when I talked to him or came home to visit? Why didn't you ever come over when I was here?"

Her eyes locked with his. "You ask a lot of questions."

A ghost of a smile curved his lips. "It's one of the things I do when I want answers. You know more about me than I know about you. You even know about the scars on my body. It's not fair. I know hardly anything about you or your body."

She wished he wouldn't touch her. It was like giving a drop of water to someone who was dying of thirst.

She was literally saved by the bell. Cabe reluctantly dropped his hand and went to answer the door.

Summer could hear several voices, one very familiar. What in the world was Celia doing here? she wondered, hurriedly standing up. It wasn't long before she found out. Cabe came back into the library, with Harry and Celia following closely behind.

Summer's friend was wearing a T-shirt maternity top announcing BABY ON BOARD. Since she was so tiny, barely five feet in height, the bulk of her tummy made her seem almost as wide as she was tall. Her blond hair was cut short, adding to the general impression of a pregnant pixie.

Her husband, Harry, was as tall and dark as Cabe, and he towered over his diminutive wife.

Celia was the first to react to the untidy condition of the library. "That's funny. I never felt the earthquake. When did it happen?" Spotting Summer, she exclaimed in mock surprise, "Hi, Summer. Fancy meeting you here."

"Especially since you knew I was going to be here," Summer said dryly.

Undeterred, Celia wound her way in and around the items on the floor. "That's why I volunteered to tag along when Harry said he was coming over tonight to see Cabe."

"Her real reason for coming over tonight," Harry explained, "was that she wanted a pizza and was hoping to talk you into getting one." Harry's amused smile faded as his gaze veered away from Summer to the clutter scattered around the room. "I see your housekeeping talents haven't improved over the years, Cabe."

Looking from Summer to Cabe and then back to Summer, Celia asked hopefully, "Are we interrupting anything?"

Summer grinned at the speculative gleam in her friend's eyes. "No. You aren't interrupting anything."

Celia's disappointment was obvious. "Darn."

Harry bent down and picked up a couple of framed pictures, one of a bareback rider and one of Hadley in his ringmaster's costume. "Have we been taking a trip down memory lane?"

"The trip is over." Cabe's gaze shifted to Summer. "It looks like we have some help putting all this stuff away. I'll order a pizza, and we'll have this room cleaned up before it's delivered."

The others exchanged glances, then started to laugh. Cabe frowned in puzzlement. "What's so funny?"

"If we wait for a pizza to be delivered," Harry said, "we'll be old and gray before it gets here. The closest pizza parlor is ten miles away in Tungston. We have to go get it."

In Chicago, Cabe thought, he could have a seven-course meal delivered to his door if he wanted it. It was another instance of the difference between his life in the city and what he could expect to have in Clearview. "If we all pitch in," he said, "we could have this room tidied up in a couple of hours, and then we'll go get a pizza, if Celia can hold out that long."

Celia was willing to wait, so long as she would get her pizza eventually. She and Harry happily began helping, following Summer's directions for where everything should go, examining, commenting, and exclaiming over each item. If they hadn't taken the time to listen to the stories about the various souvenirs, they would have been done sooner, but they wouldn't have had as much fun.

Cabe found he couldn't look away when Summer laughed at a comment from Celia. He realized it was the first time he had heard her laugh, a genuine expression of pure pleasure from deep inside her. Her eyes sparkled like green diamonds. Her husky laughter sent shivers of pleasure down his spine, and he knew he wanted to hear that sound again and again.

When the floor was clear, the two men left to get the pizzas. Celia and Summer continued working, storing the last pile of items on the furniture.

Sitting behind the desk, Celia poked through a box of campaign buttons. "The only other time I had to close up a house was when my Grandmother Hazzard moved into a nursing home. There was a big difference, though. We took all her belongings and packed them into boxes. We didn't take everything out and then put it back again. It doesn't look like Cabe knows whether he's coming or going."

Since that was an accurate description of how she herself was feeling, Summer only managed a weak smile. "You'll have to ask Cabe what his plans—"

The ringing of the telephone cut off the rest of her sentence. Celia was closer to the phone, but she relinquished that honor to Summer with a wave of her hand and delved back into the box.

"Flynn residence," Summer said. A female voice asked for Cabe, and Summer told her he wasn't there. "Could I take a message?"

The woman didn't sound pleased at being put off. "Tell Cabe to call Star as soon as he can. It's important."

The woman hung up abruptly, and Summer stared at the phone. Star?

"Bad news?" Celia asked.

Shrugging, Summer put the phone down. "I don't know. It's some woman named Star who wants Cabe to call her back."

Celia made a face. "Star?"

Summer picked up the box of campaign buttons and put it in a cupboard under one of the bookshelves. "She's probably a gorgeous blond with a smile that lights up half the windy city and a body that won't quit." She heard a snort of disgust from Celia and added, "Do you honestly think Cabe has been living like a monk in Chicago, Celia? Of course, he has women there."

"You don't seem very upset about it."

"Why should I be? It's his life."

"And the thought of some other woman in his life doesn't bother you one little bit? Pull the other leg, Summer. I've seen the way you look at him, or rather the way you try not to look at him. I know you. You're carrying a torch that could light up all of Clearview on a moonless night. You want that man, my girl."

Summer didn't try to deny it. "That's the one major difference between us, Celia. You expect to get what you want, and I don't expect anything." One corner of her mouth curved up in a facsimile of a smile. "I wanted to make the cheerleading squad, too, if you remember."

They heard the men's voices as they returned with the pizza. "Leave it alone, Celia," Summer whispered. "Don't try to do what you did when we were in the ninth grade. Johnny Petucchio didn't appreciate your feeble attempts at matchmaking, and neither will Cabe. He's leaving town soon, and I would just as soon my pride didn't go with him."

Celia stared thoughtfully at Summer. "I'll let nature take its course," she said solemnly.

"I'd appreciate that. Come on, your pizza awaits."

The men weren't in the kitchen or the dining room, but the French doors off the latter were open. They stepped outside to find that the men had set the pizza boxes on the small glass table on the patio, along with a bottle of wine and a six-pack of beer.

Summer gave Cabe the message from Star. His only reaction was a nod before he proceeded to serve the crusty, cheesy pizza onto their paper plates. He made no move to return the call from the impatient Star. Instead, he pulled out a chair for Summer, then sat down himself. Summer exchanged glances with Celia, who gave an almost imperceptible shrug of her shoulders.

While they ate the fragrant slices of pizza and sipped beer and drank wine—except for Celia who had to drink the glass of milk her husband set down in front of her—the conversation was mostly about the past, escapades Harry and Cabe had been involved in years ago or various people they had all known at some time or other. Celia contributed a few incidents from the class she and Summer had taken to become lifesavers.

"I swear I got the heaviest girl in this county as my partner," she said in mock disgust. "They dropped her off in the middle of the lake, and I was supposed to rescue her. I had to swim out to her, bring her back to shore, and carry her up onto the beach to give her artificial respiration. I nearly ruined myself lugging her out of the water. Summer, on the other hand, ended up with tiny Frannie Dunlap, whom she could have brought out with one hand tied behind her back."

"It took great skill to keep her from blowing away when I lifted her out of the water," Summer said with a broad smile.

Helping herself to a third slice of pizza, Summer looked across the table at Cabe, catching his gaze on her mouth. Suddenly self-conscious, she licked her bottom lip, removing a drop of tomato sauce left by the pizza. Something changed in his eyes, and she found she couldn't look away. Slowly he brought his gaze up to collide with hers, and she felt her heart thud in her chest.

She forgot Harry and Celia, the pizza, and would have had difficulty supplying her own name as he stared at her.

Luckily, Celia's faculties were in better working order. She knew a couple who wanted to be alone when she saw one. Nudging her husband, she faked a yawn and said, "Boy, am I bushed. It's time we were going home, Harry. It's past my bedtime."

Harry gave her a blank look. Since his wife rarely went to bed before midnight, he couldn't help wondering why she was ready to call it a night at ten o'clock. A well-aimed kick to his ankle and Celia's nod toward Summer and Cabe, who were engrossed in each other, gave him the clue. It was indeed time for them to leave.

He scooted his chair back and helped Celia to her feet. "It's been fun, but we've got to be going."

Cabe stood as well, and didn't try to talk them into staying longer. He did place his hand on Summer's shoulder as she began to push her chair away from the table, effectively stopping her. Smiling, Celia said good night to Summer and headed toward the door with Cabe and Harry.

To give herself something to do while Cabe walked his guests to the door, Summer began to clear away the remnants of their meal. She was wiping off the table when Cabe came back outside. He was carrying the bottle of wine and two glasses she had taken inside.

He poured out some wine and handed one of the glasses to her. "I don't have a porch swing, but we can sit out here and enjoy the night air."

"I should be going, Cabe. It's getting late."

"It's already too late, Summer," he said enigmatically. He pulled out a chair for her. "Stay a little longer. We haven't had much chance to talk."

Against her better judgment, Summer sat down. "If it's about the island, my week isn't up yet."

Considering what he was doing out there, the island was the last thing he wanted to discuss with her. He took the chair next to her, leaning back with his long legs stretched out in front of him. "You've got your week." He sipped his wine, then added casually, "You can have more than a week if you need it."

Summer almost choked on her wine. She coughed several times, and when she finally got her breath, she said, "I thought you were in such a hurry to get everything taken care of so you could hightail it back to the big city."

A strange smile appeared. "Some things can be done quickly, and some take a little longer."

She supposed that was true, but she didn't feel

like discussing philosophy at the moment. Apparently neither did Cabe.

"Did you and Celia really have a pie party on the island like Celia said?"

"I'm afraid so. It seemed like a good idea at the time."

"Did Hadley know about it?" He chuckled. "All Celia seemed to want to talk about was the four different pies you both ate."

"I didn't know Hadley then. We snuck over there one night in my boat. And we didn't eat all the pies. Just a little out of each one."

"Why pies?"

"We went to the bakery to get some bread to make sandwiches for our picnic, and Mrs. Diamond was taking freshly baked pies out of the oven. Somehow we forgot about the bread and chose four different pies."

He was silent for a long time as he studied her. "I would like to have known you then," he said at last. "The girl who takes pies on a picnic, who rides around the lake on a bicycle to see if she can do it in one day, and who spent every night for a week out on the lake trying to find a phantom sailboat."

"I didn't *try* to find it. I found it. It was that idiot politician's son from Saint Louis who painted his boat black and used black sails with no running lights. Weren't you paying attention when Celia mentioned that little detail?"

"Oh, I listened to every word she said about you. It was one way of finding out more about you. You don't exactly volunteer much about yourself."

His voice had changed from a conversational tone to a deeper, more intimate one that sent a tingle of awareness along her spine. She stood up and walked over to the edge of the patio where several rosebushes lined the cement border.

"Everyone in this town knows all about me," she said sharply. "All you have to do is ask them about the town drunk's daughter. They'll be more than happy to tell you how they tried to take me away from my father for my own good. I believe it was the good Preacher Johnson's wife I bit on the hand when she tried to forcibly remove me from 'the den of iniquity' I lived in."

He slowly walked over to her, stopping close behind her but not touching her like he wanted to. "What happened?" he asked softly.

Turning around, she was a little startled to find him so near, but she didn't move away. "Why all the curiosity about me? Do you want stories to tell your friends back in Chicago about the strange people you met in little Clearview?"

She was baiting him, but he didn't rise to it. "I'm asking you, Summer. Tell me what happened."

The chip of bitterness was no longer as big as it used to be, but a splinter of anger still remained, large enough to harden her voice. "If I remember correctly, I told Mrs. Johnson if she didn't leave our house, I would announce to the entire town that her darling son shared his vast collection of girlie magazines with the Boy Scouts."

Cabe chuckled. He could just see her doing it. "Am I correct in assuming she backed off?"

"Oh, yes. She sputtered for a while, but left me alone after that."

"And that's what you want, isn't it? To be left alone." Without waiting for her answer, he drew her into his arms. "I can't do that, no matter how much you may want me to, Summer. I can't leave you alone."

He pressed his lips to hers, his tongue surging into the soft heat of her mouth. His hands had a will of their own, sliding over her body, arousing and caressing, absorbing the vibrant warmth of her. Taking her mouth, tasting her essence wasn't enough. He needed to take all of her, to taste all of her.

Answering his kiss passionately, Summer gave in to the throbbing pleasure of desire. Her body melted into his, her hands gripping his waist as he took her on a journey of sensuality.

"Hold me," he murmured against her mouth. "I need to feel your hands on me."

Like a puppet, she lifted her arms to do his bidding. As her hands grazed over his shoulders and around his neck, she felt his muscles contract. His hips surged against her lower body, leaving her no doubt as to how her nearness was affecting him. She was amazed she could elicit such a powerful response from him, but then a small doubt filtered through the haze of passion to remind her that an experienced, virile man like Cabe had held many women in his arms . . . like the sultry-sounding Star she had spoken to on the phone.

Cabe felt her withdrawal, even though he still held her tightly in his arms. He waited as she slowly raised her lashes to look up at him. A myriad of emotions flickered in the depths of her eyes, and he wondered at the wariness mixed with desire. She still didn't fully trust him. Or was it herself she didn't trust? He just hoped he could give her the time she apparently needed. The way his body was aching, he was going to have another rough night, as long and lonely and sleepless as the last couple of evenings.

His knuckles grazed the smooth skin of her cheek as his mouth curved in a faint imitation of a smile. He took a deep breath, his chest pressing against her delicious breasts. That didn't help his attempt to control the violent hunger in his body. "I know. I'm rushing you."

She felt he deserved her honesty since she couldn't give him anything else. "I've never wanted anyone like this before."

He could have told her he knew that, but didn't. She was insecure enough without having him throw her inexperience in her face—even though he could also have told her that her instinctive responses to him were more satisfying to his ego than the sexual expertise practiced by some women he had known in the past.

"But?" he asked.

She stepped back, relieved when he dropped his arms to allow her to move away from him. "But you'll only be here a short time, and I'm not the type who likes to be loved and left."

"I know."

She reached out to stroke a rosebud. A dash of disappointment quenched her vague hope of being more to him than a momentary attraction. Cabe recognized the desire for what it was, the pull of the senses as old as time, as elemental as lightning. It was about time she admitted what it was and let it go. She wondered how Star would handle this situation. Her mouth twisted as she bent to inhale the scent of the partially opened rose. The woman would be sophisticated and worldly, able to accept or reject a man's advances easily, not floundering around like a stranded guppy.

She exclaimed softly when a thorn pricked her finger. She automatically raised her finger to her mouth, but Cabe's hand stopped her. Her lips parted slightly in wonder as he brought her finger up to his mouth and his tongue soothed her soft skin.

"It's only a scratch," she said breathlessly.

"It's one hurt too many." His fingers threaded through hers, and he led her toward the French doors. "And I'm not going to add to it."

Before she knew what had happened, Summer was escorted to her Jeep, kissed hard and quick, then gently stuffed behind the wheel.

Cabe bent down to speak through the open window. "I'll see you tomorrow."

Her eyes searched his, but she was unable to read his expression. His fingers tightened on the window frame, then he straightened up. "Leave while I can still let you go, Summer."

All of her movements were automatic as she drove away. It was a good thing she knew the way home so well and could drive without thinking about where she was going.

It was frightening to realize she hadn't really left Cabe at all. An essential part of her had remained with him.

Her heart.

Six

If people noticed the evidence of a sleepless night, they tactfully didn't mention it to her. The sunglasses Summer wore when she ventured out of her office hid the shadows under her eyes, but other signs of exhaustion were apparent. Although she was usually even-tempered, today she met the slightest mistake made by her staff with a sharp comment. She moved as though weights were attached to her legs and she remained behind her desk more than usual, letting her young crew handle the tourists without her guidance.

Theresa, who kept the office humming along efficiently, didn't bother Summer with minor questions. After working at the marina for three summers, the older woman knew the answers to most questions posed by the tourists, so unless one of the boathouses burned down, she left Summer alone.

Considering it was a Saturday, one of the busiest days at the marina, her lack of interest was obvious and noticeable to her employees. Concerned glances were exchanged and shoulders were shrugged, but she was given what she wanted most, her privacy.

It was just as well she was safely behind the walls of her office when Jacob noticed his tools were still missing. He gave the walls of the boathouse a blasting of profanity, loud and blistering enough to take the paint off the interior if there had been any. She was also blissfully unaware that Cabe had again rented one of the boats for a return trip to the island, taking Jacob's tools with him.

This time he returned earlier than on the other day, but just as grimy and greasy. Bringing the tools with him, he hurried into the boathouse instead of going to his car. So far he had managed to evade Summer, but his luck could run out any minute. As soon as he entered the boathouse, he was confronted by a far from friendly mechanic who stood solidly in his path with both of his hands clamped to his hips.

Leaving out the colorful dialogue, the gist of Jacob's harangue dealt with how he felt about anyone other than himself working on any of the boats. Cabe didn't try to placate Jacob, but let him rattle on while he cleaned off the tools at one of the workbenches against the wall. Nodding his head occasionally to let Jacob know he was listening, he rubbed the machine oil and grease off the wrenches, then moved on to the screwdriver. Jacob warned him not to fool around with any of the boats, declaring they were his responsibility and Summer's property. No one messed around with them but him, and Mr. Flynn better understand that right now.

By the time Cabe was through polishing the tools, Jacob had run out of breath and swearwords. He continued to stand nearby, though, to guard against Cabe taking any of his equipment again.

"Take it easy, Jacob," Cabe said. "I'm not going to do anything to hurt your tools or the boats."

"How about Miss Roberts?"

The quiet question brought Cabe's attention to the older man's face. Because of the concern in the mechanic's eyes, he began to explain to Jacob exactly what he had been doing with the tools. When he finished, he was amazed to see the difference a smile could make on Jacob's craggy features.

"I'll be damned," Jacob exclaimed. "Miss Roberts is going to be surprised, all right."

"I just hope she'll be pleasantly surprised. She's pretty possessive about the island, especially the carousel. She may not like me playing around with it."

"It's hard to say which way women will jump," Jacob mumbled, scratching his head. "I ain't never figured that out, and I'm a lot older than you."

Cabe smiled. "Where is she now?"

"She's holed up in her office. Been there all day."

"All day?"

Jacob nodded.

"Isn't that a little usual?"

"Yup, but them women can get funny notions sometimes. That's why I work with boats."

"I've found timing is very important when dealing with women, Jacob," Cabe said, wiping his hands on a clean rag. "And this isn't the time to let Summer see me like this. Is there any way I can get to my car in the parking lot without her seeing me from her office?"

Jacob gave him directions. Cabe nodded, then asked one more favor. "After I clean up, I'm going back out to the island and this is what I would like you to do . . ."

• • •

After everyone had left for the day, Summer couldn't think of another thing that had to be done. She was tidying up her desk when Jacob pushed open the outside door and ambled back toward her office. It was so unusual for him to come to the front office, she jumped up and asked anxiously, "What's wrong, Jacob?"

"Nothing's wrong," he mumbled uncomfortably. "I just thought you might like to know the guy who took out the *Bluebird* is marooned on the island and can't get back."

"How do you know that?"

He shrugged, looking down at the floor rather than meeting her eyes. "I guess he must have yelled at somebody as they sailed by the island. All I know is somebody's got to go get him and tow the boat back."

Summer sighed heavily. "You'll have to come with me, Jacob. Everyone else has left. We'll take the *Falcon*. It's faster and you prefer a speedboat to a sailboat."

She half-expected Jacob to refuse to go with her, but he didn't. He walked along beside her, silent and stoic all the way to the dock. He automatically got behind the controls of the boat while she untied the ropes without giving her the choice. He didn't trust anyone to pilot a boat except himself.

Five minutes later he shut off the engine and let the boat coast up to the dock jutting out from the island. The missing sailboat was secured to the other side of the dock with the sail down. At first glance, there didn't seem to be anything wrong with it. There was no sign of the stranded boater anywhere on the dock or the shore.

Summer tied the bowline to one of the dock posts, then caught the stern line Jacob threw to her. As she was securing it, a strange sound filled the air. It was foreign to the normal light cadences, yet there was something familiar and vaguely haunting about it.

She jerked her head around to look at Jacob. "Do you hear that? The guy is having a party. He took his radio with him. At least it'll be easier for us to find him."

Jacob had followed Cabe's instructions, including telling fibs to his employer, but that was as far as he was going. "You best go find him."

She frowned. "Aren't you coming with me?"

"No."

Well, she thought with irritation. That was plain enough. Apparently Jacob preferred to stay with the boat while she got to go hunting for the stranded tourist. Fine. Great. Let him sit there all comfy cosy while she tripped all over the island looking for this guy who hadn't the sense of a flea.

"All right. Throw me the flashlight."

With the stream of light directed on the ground in front of her, she left the dock and headed in the direction of the music. She had gone about twenty feet into the trees when she suddenly stopped.

That wasn't a radio she was hearing, she realized in astonishment. That was the distinctive sounds of a calliope. "But that can't be," she said to the trees around her. The only ride with a calliope was the carousel, and it hadn't worked for years.

She wove in and around the trees and bushes. The closer she got to the area where the carousel was, the better she could see bright light filtering through the trees. The tinkling music got louder. Her step slowed as she came nearer. Then, edging around the ring-toss booth, she stopped.

All she could do was stare. Hundreds of lightbulbs whirled around and around as the stately horses pranced up and down, revolving with the carousel. She felt as though she had been transported to a fantasy land. Slowly she moved forward.

The flashlight dropped from her hand as she walked toward the magical vision in front of her. A black horse caught her eye. Actually it was the person sitting on the black horse who had her staring in disbelief.

She watched in fascination as Cabe and the wooden horse revolved out of her sight. She was standing in the same spot when they came around again.

This time Cabe casually gestured for her to join him.

Suddenly, as though a spring had snapped to release her, she ran toward the turning wooden platform and jumped aboard. Cabe was several horses away, and she wove her way through the pairs of horses till she reached him.

Her eyes were shining as she gazed up at him. His maroon windbreaker was open in the front to reveal a white cotton shirt. Her hand rested on his muscular thigh without her actually thinking about what she was doing.

His dark eyes dwelled on the contours of her face, the brilliance of her eyes. The hours of sweaty, greasy work were worth it just to see the joy in her eyes. "Care to go riding with me?"

"Yes."

When the horse was in the low position, he lifted her onto it so that she was sitting sidesaddle between the brass pole and his body. "Where would you like to go?"

Sliding her hands under his jacket to his waist, she tilted her head back in order to see his face clearly. "Anywhere. Everywhere. Wherever you're going."

He was spellbound by the look of supreme happiness in her eyes, feeling an unfamiliar gratification in being the one who had given her so much pleasure. "We'll just keep going until we get there."

"I feel like it's Christmas, Fourth of July, and New Year's Eve all rolled up into one special night." Her voice was husky with emotion. "Thank you, Cabe."

He thought of all the times in the past he had given a woman a gift. There had been flowers, jewelry, perfume, each handed out as social tokens because they were expected. Yet none of his presents had been accepted with such natural, heartfelt joy.

He looked around at the lights and the graceful horses. "At first I began to work on the engine for Hadley. Then it was because the carousel meant so much to you. Toward the end, I discovered I was doing it for me as well."

After all he had done, she hated to ask, but she needed to know the answer. "Does that mean you've changed your mind about wanting to sell the island?"

His gaze returned to her. "I don't know. To be perfectly honest, Summer, I just don't know. A lot has happened in a short time, and I haven't really had the time to figure everything out yet. I've put most decisions on hold until I can decide exactly what to do." He smiled. "This isn't a night for serious conversation. There are no tomorrows, no yesterdays. This is never-never land. There's just now. Just you and me."

"Do you think it can really be that easy?"

"Why not? We can make tonight whatever we want."

Pressed tightly against his warm body with the lights and music of the carousel swirling around her, she thought she already had everything she could possibly want. It was more than she ever thought she would have.

"And what do you want?" she asked.

His gaze dropped to her mouth. "Are you sure you want me to answer that?"

She smiled boldly at him. "I'm not worried. There isn't a lot you can do on the back of a horse."

He accepted her statement as a challenge. "You don't think so?"

"There's no brass ring to reach for."

"That's true, but there are other things to reach for." He proved the point by lowering his hand to stroke her thigh from her knee to the edge of her shorts. His slow, sensual smile acknowledged the sudden catch of her breath and the growing awareness in her eyes.

"I see what you mean," she murmured.

His thumb edged under the hem of her shorts. "Feel what I mean."

"Cabe," she gasped. "We're on a horse, for crying out loud."

"I know where we are and I know what I'm doing," he said with amusement.

Grasping at the first excuse she could come up with, she said, "Jacob is waiting for me at the dock. He'll wonder where I am."

The thumb was joined by his other fingers, finding the bare flesh under the elastic of her panties. "Jacob isn't there, Summer."

"Yes, he is," she said as indignantly as she could, considering the fact that the simple act of breathing wasn't as easy as it should have been. "He thought someone was stranded on the island and—"

Interrupting gently, Cabe repeated his earlier statement as his hand spread out over the fullness of her upper thigh. "He isn't there."

It was difficult to think coherently when he was touching her where no man had ever touched her before. "Why wouldn't he be there?" she managed to ask.

His fingers tightened slightly as if he expected her to pull away from him. "I told him to bring you here and then leave."

"You—you told Jacob to . . ." she sputtered wildly. Collecting herself, she tried again. "What are you saying? That I've been set up?"

"That's a rather harsh way of putting it."

Her hands went to his chest. "Then put it the way it is."

"I wanted to surprise you, and Jacob was willing to go along with my plan to get you to the island."

Summer didn't know what astonished her more, that this whole thing had been prearranged or that Jacob was Cabe's accomplice. She had never known Jacob to do anything for anyone else on a personal level. "I don't know what to say."

"Good. It's about time."

Placing his hands on either side of her face, he lowered his head to find her mouth in a hard, hungry kiss. The rising and falling of the carousel horse intensified the pressure of his mouth against hers in a rhythmic, undulating movement. His hands moved down to her waist, he shifted her legs so that they lay over his thigh and her back was to the pole, bringing her breasts fully against his chest.

His voice was husky and low. "Hold on to me. We're going for a long ride."

Her hands slid around to his back under his jacket. There was really no danger of her falling off, since he was holding her tightly. His mouth tantalized and devoured, no longer teasing or testing but aggressively demanding a response from her. If she ever let go of him, she felt as though she would fly off the earth, spinning into infinity. He was heat and smoke, burning her and smothering her with his touch, his taste.

Cabe captured her lips once more, needing the intimate contact, wanting so much more. Keeping his control tightly reined, he allowed one hand to stroke down her throat and over her shoulder. Her warmth seeped into his palms through her shirt, enticing him to find other pleasures. Gently but firmly he tugged the tail of her shirt from her shorts, then slipped his hands beneath it, smoothing over her ribcage, stopping when he found the soft feminine mounds of flesh covered by a bit of lace.

Summer murmured something against his mouth. It could have been his name or a promise, but she knew it wasn't a protest. There were no longer choices to make or time for thinking about what she was doing. There were just sensations. Glorious, mindless pleasure.

The carousel spun on. The horses continued their leaps and landings, oblivious to the passion stirring in the couple who rode a black charger. The days of children dropping cotton candy onto their manes and dabbing ice cream into their shiny, painted coats were over. Tonight's passengers had more adult matters on their minds.

Cabe suddenly broke his mouth away from hers, his hand freezing on her breast. What in hell did he think he was doing? he wondered crazily, gazing down at her. Did he think he could make love to her on the back of a moving horse, for Pete's sake? He blinked several times as if he were coming out of a drugged sleep, trying to focus on the woman in his arms.

His smile was somewhat ragged around the edges as he gently withdrew his hand. "If we go any further, we're going to have a riding accident. Maybe when I was a few years younger, I could have managed it, but not now."

Summer felt she was coming to the surface of a deep sea after nearly drowning. Her eyes were wide and vulnerable as she met his dark gaze.

Her own smile was weak. "It might be embarrassing to have to explain how we broke our necks necking."

He made a face, clearly disapproving of her choice of words. "Necking is what teenagers do in the backseat of a car. What we shared was a preliminary to making love. I stopped because I'd rather wait until we can get to a soft bed."

His calm assumption shook her. He was taking it for granted she would automatically go along with his plans once they found the bed. She had to admit he had reason to feel that way. She hadn't exactly beaten him off with a stick.

She waited until the horse made its descent, then jumped down onto the wooden platform. "It's time to get off the merry-go-round and back to the real world."

He swung his leg over the saddle and slid off the horse. Resting his forearms casually on her shoulders, he studied her face. "This *is* the real world, Summer. What we have between us is very real. You might as well accept it. I have."

"What's real is you will be returning to Chicago and I will be staying here, Cabe. That's what I've accepted."

He continued to watch her. She was saying she wasn't available for a brief one-night stand, which was all she thought he was offering. Well? he asked himself. Wasn't that exactly what he wanted? Wasn't it? His conscience had never been a problem in the past. He had always shied away from any permanent involvement, and one certainly didn't fit in with his plans for the future now.

This woman wasn't going to be easy to leave behind, he realized. And taking her would be the biggest mistake he ever made. Making love with her would get rid of one ache but might create another.

What in bloody hell was wrong with him? he asked himself for about the hundredth time since he had arrived in Clearview. He stared down at Summer as though the answer could be found in the depths of her lovely eyes. It wasn't going to be that simple. The answers could only be found within himself.

Dropping his arms away from her, he changed the subject. "I'll show you how to start the engine so that you can use the carousel whenever you want."

Summer didn't immediately reply. She couldn't switch her feelings on and off like a light switch, as he seemed to do. How could he kiss her with such passion and then calmly talk about engines? she wondered in amazement. Then she answered her own question. Because a few kisses hadn't meant anything to him. He had been looking for a diversion, and she was handy. It had been an unforgettable night in many ways, she thought, but it was time to stop the music. The party was over.

"This has been wonderful, Cabe, but we should go. The lights and music may create some curiosity among the people who live near the island. I don't want anyone coming here."

"All right. We'll shut it down. Come with me so that I can show you how to make it work."

Standing next to him in front of the panel of controls, Summer paid attention to his instructions, although she doubted she would ever use the information. The memories of this night would be too vivid, too powerful to live with if she came back to ride the carousel after he had gone. She didn't want to remember how he had made her feel, how his touch could make her ache.

When the carousel was turned off, the darkness and silence settled around them like a cloak. Cabe had the flashlight and flicked it on so that they could find their way back to the boat.

He held out his hand. "Come on, Tinkerbell. It's time to leave never-never land."

Placing her hand in his, she attempted to meet his bantering tone with one of her own. "Does that make you Peter Pan or Captain Hook?"

He helped her from the platform onto the ground. "Since there's a dispute as to whether Peter Pan was a boy or a girl, I'll opt for being myself. I know which one I am."

Summer decided not to touch that remark. She, too, knew what he was, a man who was danger- ous to her peace of mind.

Both were silent as they followed the path down to the dock. Cabe had been right. The speedboat was no longer tied up there. Summer stepped into the sailboat first and hoisted the sail while Cabe untied the lines. He pushed off and took the oar to propel the boat out far enough to catch some wind, such as there was. Because she had come to the island in a motorboat, Summer hadn't noticed the lack of wind. Now she did. The full moon gave them plenty of light to see their way across the lake, and once the sails caught enough breeze, they skimmed slowly over the water with Summer at the helm.

When they were nearing the marina, Cabe shifted over to sit next to her, still holding the jib rope. He bent down to murmur in her ear. "Don't head in yet."

"If we don't, we'll have to row back. There isn't much wind."

"Then I'll row back."

She hesitated to do as he asked. It was tempting to prolong the evening, but like most temptations, there was a good chance the indulgence would be regretted later, like the time she ate three caramel apples and had a bellyache for days. Being with Cabe caused a different ache, one she was afraid would never go away.

Turning her head enough to see his face, she thought she saw an odd vulnerability there. He appeared to be struggling with something, and she didn't flatter herself it had anything to do with her. Instinctively she felt he needed the wide expanses of water to counteract whatever was crowding him. It was a feeling she had experienced herself when life had piled on a load of problems.

It took her only a few seconds to lower the sail and resume her seat in the stern. The smaller jib sail fluttered limply when Cabe released the rope. The boat was gradually becalmed, with the moonlight shining down on the almost calm surface of the lake.

It wasn't in Summer's nature to invade anyone else's privacy. She prized her own so highly, the last thing she would do was probe into Cabe's. She sat quietly looking out over the lake as she had many times before, listening to the soft sounds of the water lapping gently against the sides of the boat. She couldn't help but wonder what his more sophisticated women in Chicago, like the infamous Star, would say under these circumstances.

Whether it was the calming effect of the water or the undemanding company of the woman sitting near him, Cabe felt his tension peel away like old paint. The strain of dealing with the death of his grandfather and the subsequent responsibilities had been thrown in his lap at a bad time. His dissatisfaction with his life in Chicago had already been draining him, making him restless. The restlessness was nothing like the usual itch he had lived with, the need to be doing something, to be going somewhere, on the move with his work, his life. Since he had been back in Clearview, he felt as though brakes had been put on his feet, slowing him down long enough for him to look within himself.

He wasn't sure he liked what he saw.

He was beginning to wonder if Summer hadn't been right about him. Perhaps he was a selfish bastard. God knows, he had always done as he pleased regarding his work, his friends, his relationships with women. Facing life on his own terms had worked for ten years, but for some reason it wasn't enough anymore.

And he didn't know what to do about it.

He shifted his gaze from the water to the woman sitting a short distance away. The moonlight grazed her skin, highlighting the delicate contours of her face. There was a serenity about her that called to a hidden part of him he hadn't known existed. He couldn't imagine any other woman he knew who would be satisfied with simply being there with him. No, he reconsidered. Summer was there *for* him, as Hadley had been. She seemed to accept him the way he was without trying to change him or challenge him or demand anything from him. She had no idea how rare that was to a man.

"Summer?"

His voice roused her from her own thoughts. She met his dark gaze without saying a word.

A rush of tenderness flowed through him, overwhelming him like a tide covering the shore. "I've never met a woman like you before," he said huskily.

Her years of defensiveness made her straighten her spine and reply dryly, "No, I don't imagine you have."

Somehow he had offended her, and it was the last thing he wanted to do. "I meant I've never known a woman who says as little as you do. Usually I can tell what a woman is thinking within the first fifteen minutes of meeting her. I've known you almost a week and I still don't know what makes you tick."

"You make me sound like a clock."

"Oh, I know you're a woman. A desirable, warm woman with silky hair and satin skin. A woman whose rare smile tightens my guts with an ache that is both pain and pleasure. I've caressed the outer Summer, but I've yet to touch the inner woman because you won't let me in. You remind me of a velvet cactus, soft yet prickly."

His whimsical description made her smile. "I've been called a lot of things, but never a velvet cactus."

"But you've been labeled in other ways?"

Her gaze returned to the lake. "I suppose I have. 'A workaholic,' 'belligerent,' 'combative.' 'Brat' has been applied to me a number of times to my face and, I imagine, many more times behind my back, probably with good reason. I remember one of my teachers saying I was pugnacious, and I had to look that up in a dictionary when I got home. The most common tag I wore for years was the town drunk's daughter. I've punched out one or two kids who taunted me with that one. Of course, they were only repeating what they'd heard their parents say, but I didn't know that at the time."

Cabe examined her profile and wondered how large the chip on her shoulder had been. Comparing her early years with his own, he knew how lucky he had been. He had lost his parents, but he had had Hadley and a safe, secure upbringing without prejudice coloring his view of life. Thinking back, he could recall the occasional disparaging remark about Gene Roberts not being able to hold his liquor. At the time, he had never given any thought to the child he had seen holding her father's hand as he weaved out of a bar downtown. He had also noticed her around the marina, pumping gas when she was barely able to reach the nozzle and lugging around equipment almost bigger than she was.

"Did Hadley ever tell you about the time the circus was run out of a town in Ohio?" he asked.

"No, he didn't. He must have missed that one."

"A carnival had been in a small town before Hadley's circus was scheduled and had rooked the people out of a lot of money. A couple of impressionable teenage girls had run off with a couple of roustabouts. Hadley's circus was painted with the same brush, and they weren't able to pound in one stake before the local authorities showed up with every warrant imaginable. Those people acted out of fear and ignorance, thinking all circus types were alike. The people of Clearview treated your father the same way because they didn't understand his problem."

"They didn't try either."

"Is that why you stay in Clearview? Are you the hairshirt the town has to wear as a punishment for the way they treated your father?"

Placing a life-preserver cushion on the deck, Summer made herself more comfortable. "I stay here because I have nowhere else to go. I support myself and a few others by keeping the marina operating. It's taken me a long time, but I've been able to put the past where it belongs. Hadley once said dwelling on the regrets of the past saps a person's energy for getting on with the present. I agree with him."

She wrapped her arms around her knees. "What about you, Cabe? Do you have any regrets?"

He threw several more cushions down on the deck and sat down beside her. "Everyone has regrets. Some bigger than others." He paused, then said, "I think my biggest regret is that I had to let you go when we were on the carousel."

Summer became still. Her arms loosened from around her knees and dropped to her sides.

He brushed several strands of hair away from her face. "I can't use you, Summer. As badly as I want you, I won't take advantage of you by making love to you for all the wrong reasons. It's important to me for you to understand that."

"I haven't understood a thing since you came back to Clearview, Cabe," she said. "What would the right reasons be to make love?"

He lowered his hand to cup the back of her neck. "You aren't the kind of woman to take lightly, Summer. You're the type men marry, not play around with."

"And that's all you want to do is play. No long-term relationships, no ties that bind you down." She smiled gently. "I know that, Cabe. I don't remember asking for any commitment from you."

His grip tightened. "No, you haven't, but that doesn't mean you don't require one. I've got enough on my mind without adding guilt for forcing you into something you don't want."

A thread of anger wove through her. "How do you know what I want?"

"What you think you want," he corrected her.

"No," she said emphatically. "I know what I want or don't want. I've been on my own a long time, Cabe. I know my own mind. Not all of my choices have been the right ones, but they were mine to make. If you don't want to make love with me, that's your decision, but don't say it's because you think you would be forcing me against my will."

Cabe felt pulled in two different directions, wanting her with every fiber of his being yet feeling he should protect her. His iron will was slowly eroding to mush. She had openly admitted she wanted him, and his resolve to leave her alone was weakening.

Summer frowned at him. "This is a stupid conversation."

She scrambled to her feet and moved toward the sail. When she lifted her arms to raise the sail, her shirt became taut across her breasts, giving Cabe a clear profile of her curves. He felt his body tighten and the last of his good intentions faded away.

He rose to his knees and put out his hand to halt her. "You're right. Maybe we should stop talking altogether."

He pulled her down to her knees facing him. A sudden tension sparked between them, like the electricity in the air before a heavy storm.

Summer slowly released the breath she had been holding. "You've changed your mind," she whispered.

He plunged his fingers through her hair to cup the back of her head. "I don't have a mind. You've made me lose it."

He kissed her desperately, hungrily, as if he needed that contact with her or he would go mad. Breaking open her lips, his tongue surged between her teeth as his hands slid down her back to her bottom, bringing her lower body into the cradle of his hips. The soft yearning sound she made into his mouth snapped the thin thread of his control, and he lowered her onto the cushions on the deck.

Keeping the bulk of his weight off her, he partially covered her body with his, inserting one of his legs between hers as he concentrated on his claim on her mouth. Each movement of her lips under his, the way she moved her hips against his, was driving him beyond sanity.

"Put your arms around me, Summer," he said hoarsely. "I need to feel you touch me."

Sliding her hand under his shirt, she found the warmth of his bare skin. She ran her palms over his waist and across his back, feeling his muscles contract beneath her touch. When he trembled against her, she arched her hips and tightened her arms as a wave of drowning sensations crashed over her.

Unable to wait any longer, Cabe deftly removed her shorts and pushed off her shirt before tugging at his own clothing. Even in his haste, he forced himself to come down to her slowly, covering her gradually with his heated flesh, letting her get used to his weight, to his claim on her body. Savoring every inch of her satin skin and luscious curves, he devoured her with his eyes and his hands and his mouth His blood thundered in his head and hardened his body until he thought he would explode in a storm of passion.

To his amazement, she pulled him down fully on her and kissed him wildly. She didn't want him to be kind and considerate. She wanted him, all of him, now, immediately and desperately.

Husky laughter escaped him, and he looked down at her exultantly. He had never felt satisfaction in knowing a woman wanted him. Lord knows, he wanted her with a need deeper and more potent than he thought possible to feel.

"I should give you more time," he said, his voice low and rough, "but I can't, not now."

Her eyes held his as she parted her legs in response. She had given him her answer in a way that spoke more clearly than any words she could have said.

Unable to look away, Cabe felt himself sinking into the green depths of her eyes as he moved to forge his body with hers. Shock ran along his spine when her eyes flickered as he met the resistance he hadn't expected to find. He froze, unable to believe what was crashing into his brain.

She felt him begin to withdraw, and her arms became bands of steel holding him to her as she completed their union with a strong thrust of her hips. This time she didn't flinch.

"Summer," he choked out. His body failed to resist the heat of hers as it closed round him. A sense of urgency swallowed him in a whirlpool of fevered passion, and he took her with him on the sensual journey.

Summer's hands clenched against his back as she was carried to a place of delirious pleasure. She was aware of an odd sensation deep inside her as though her body was a tightened spring. The spring suddenly exploded, casting her into ecstasy. She gasped his name, and he answered with a final powerful surge of his body.

They lay together for a long time, wrapped in each other's arms as they returned slowly to reality. The only sound was the occasional ripple of water against the sides of the boat and their labored breathing.

Cabe finally raised his head from her shoulder. "Are you all right?" he asked, concerned.

Her soft smile spread a warm glow through him. "I'm fine."

"I hurt you. I'm sorry, Summer. I didn't realize it would be your first time."

He began to move off her, but she wouldn't let him. "I have no regrets, Cabe. I don't want you to have any either. If you did, it would diminish what we shared and that would really hurt me more than the minor discomfort of being deflowered." She framed his face in her hands. "I'm glad it was you."

His chest tightened painfully as though a fist were clutching his heart. He was overwhelmed with a tenderness for this quixotic woman who had given him more than her body.

Still deep inside her, he could feel himself harden and saw the startled awareness enter her eyes. A corner of his mouth curved into a slow smile. "Does this feel like regret?"

She moved her head back and forth on the cushion. "It feels like heaven."

Heaven or hell, he couldn't resist it. It was too soon for her, but cutting off his arm would be easier than stopping the headlong rush of fathomless passion.

Seven

When the world righted itself once again, they
dove over the side of the boat to cool their heated
skin. After swimming around for a brief spell, Cabe
pulled her into his arms, reveling in the feel of her
wet body fitting to his so naturally.

He wanted her again, and was astonished at
the depth of his need so soon after being inside
her. Now he knew it was a craving that would
never go away.

When she shivered under his hands, he released
her. "Let's go back to the boat. You're cold."

They dressed quickly as the wind began to pick
up, chilling them. There was enough breeze to fill
the sail once it was hoisted, and they were able to
make their way back to shore without having to
resort to rowing.

Cabe manned the tiller with Summer seated on
the deck between his thighs. He played lazily with
her hair with his free hand, enjoying the simple
pleasure of having her hand rest intimately on his
thigh.

If it were up to Summer, the *Bluebird* could

keep slicing through the water forever, but the shoreline came closer and closer with each passing minute. The night had been full of magic, fantasy, passion, and, on her side at least, love. She didn't want the night to end, but it was time to wake up and put the dreams aside. Cabe had given her more memories than she'd thought she would ever have. She would bring them out to keep her company after Cabe returned to Chicago.

Cabe's fingers stilled in her hair as they neared the dock. She could feel a tension emanating from him that hadn't been there a few minutes ago, and she wondered if he was reluctant to return to dry land too.

He was. "I'm tempted to just keep sailing," he said, "but I wouldn't want Jacob coming after me with a boat hook."

"He'd come after the boat, not you."

"I'd rather not put him to the test."

His hand grazed along her neck on its way to her shoulder. It slipped beneath her shirt and didn't stop until his fingertips rested on the upper slope of her breast. Against his thumb, he could feel the heartbeat in her throat accelerate, aware that his own was none too steady either.

"Now I know why Disneyland is so popular," he said, staring at the approaching dock. "There's something to be said for living in a fantasy world."

"Even Disneyland closes at the end of the day."

She had spoken so softly, he had had to bend down to hear what she said. He knew what she meant. Nothing had changed. The problems were still there. They had a brief respite, but now it was back to reality in all its forms. Decisions had to be made.

Once the boat was pulled up on the shore, he held her close to his side as he walked her to her cabin. Tall hedges had been planted to give protection from the north wind, but also to conceal and separate the cabin from the rest of the marina complex. He would never have found the small opening on his own. One section of shrubbery was a few feet in front of another, leaving a gap large enough to pass through.

Summer unlocked her door and flicked on the inside light. She was about to enter the cabin when Cabe's hand stopped her. Startled, she turned to look at him. She had expected him to come in with her, but apparently he had other ideas. She tried to hide the disappointment pressing down on her.

"You're going home," she said flatly.

He nodded, a strained expression in his eyes and around his mouth. "Could you take some time off tomorrow? I know Sunday is a busy day at the marina, but I'd like to spend some time with you."

He didn't sound overly enthusiastic, and she hesitated before replying. "Most of the boats are checked out early and come back late. Unless something comes up, I have less to do between ten and four if you want to give me a call during that time."

He shoved his hands into the pockets of his jacket, clenching them into fists. He didn't dare touch her or he wouldn't leave, and he knew he had to be alone. She had given him a lot to think about tonight, and he'd already had a full quota of other problems to settle.

Leaning forward, he kissed her briefly. For a few long moments, he looked down at her, aware of the hurt and confusion in her eyes. He felt like a royal bastard for leaving her so abruptly without an explanation, but he didn't know what to say to her to make it any easier for her to understand. Hell, he thought explosively. *He* didn't understand why he was leaving, so why would she? He just knew he had to be alone. He was feeling crowded and edgy, wanting her as much, no, more than he had before. It was impossible to think when he was with her.

He turned away and started down the steps. Then he stopped. She was still standing in the doorway when he looked back.

"I'll call you tomorrow, Summer."

After a significant pause she nodded.

A muscle in his jaw clenched. "I *will* call."

She nodded again.

Irritated with her silence and himself, he stomped back up the steps and clasped her shoulders roughly. "I know what you're thinking, but you're wrong. Tonight wasn't just a one-night stand, Summer. Tonight was the beginning, not the end."

She tried to wrench away from him, but without any success. "You're hurting me, Cabe."

He made the effort to loosen his grip on her. "I'm trying very hard not to hurt you, Summer. I have my reasons for leaving you tonight, and I'm not ready to tell you what they are." Especially since he didn't know what they were. His hands came up to cup her face. "You have no reason to trust me, but that's what I'm asking you to do."

She didn't have a choice, she thought. He was leaving anyway, whether she trusted him or whether she thought he was only letting her down gently. She removed his hands by gripping his wrists.

"You don't owe me any explanations, Cabe. I'm a big girl now. I knew what I was doing. No regrets, remember?" She smiled faintly. "I had a wonderful time."

He studied her face carefully, but could find no indication of how she was really feeling. She was saying all the right things, yet he couldn't help feeling she was telling him what she thought he wanted to hear.

She turned toward her door. "Thank you for fixing the carousel, Cabe." Then she went inside, closing the door behind her.

He stared at the door, then turned away.

Inside the cabin, Summer finally pushed herself away from the door. She turned off the light and walked into her small bedroom. Her movements were listless, unusually awkward and disjointed as she removed her clothes and went into her bathroom to shower.

Later as she was toweling herself dry, she happened to glance into the mirror above the sink. She frowned. *You're greedy, Tinkerbell,* she admonished her reflection. *What did you expect? Promises of undying devotion? Grow up. You had more from him than you ever expected to have.*

As she slipped a powder-blue nightgown over her head, she thought about the past and how she had learned to accept things that couldn't be changed: no mother, her father's drinking, the lack of money. She had made adjustments and gotten on with her life as best she could. She would do the same when Cabe said good-bye.

Sliding between the sheets, she punched her pillow several times as though the innocent bag of feathers were responsible for her present plight. She could hear the gentle rustle of the oak leaves outside her open window, disturbed by the wind blowing off the lake. Over the years she had stared up at this same ceiling; planning, hoping, and worrying about so many different things. Cabe had entered into those conversations with herself many times, but only in a hazy way, like when she held a seashell to her ear and visualized the ocean. He had been a nebulous figure in her imagination for so long, someone who had been in her game of "What If." It had been a harmless diversion to counteract the many responsibilities she had to deal with.

He was no longer a fantasy figure in her mind, but very real in a way she never thought he would be. He was her lover.

The following day started like most Sundays, with a line of tourists checking out boats and equipment. There was gas to be pumped; there were meals to be served in the restaurant, and souvenirs to be sold in the gift shop. Business was as usual.

Summer went about her activities wearing a beeper on her belt whenever she was out of the office. She'd left instructions that she be notified immediately when Cabe Flynn called her. The beeper never went off.

The marina closed at six, and the staff had left by six-thirty. Jacob was still in the boathouse working on an engine, but he always set his own hours and didn't need any supervision.

Summer had been sitting behind her desk since everyone had clocked out for the day, most of the time staring at the phone. The silent phone.

When it rang a little after seven, she picked it up before the first ring. "Hello?"

"Myra? How are you, babe?"

She didn't recognize the voice and she certainly wasn't Myra. "You have the wrong number."

"Come on, Myra. Quit fooling around. I know I should have called you earlier, but the guys came over and—"

"I really don't care what you and the guys did. I'm not Myra." She crashed the receiver back down.

She waited ten more minutes, then lifted the phone and punched out a familiar number. After two rings, a woman answered.

"Flynn residence."

"Hello, Adela. Could I speak to Cabe, please?"

"I'm sorry, Miss Roberts, but he's not here. He left for Chicago early this morning."

Summer almost dropped the phone. Then she clutched it so tightly, her knuckles turned white. Shock kept her silent for a long time, then she finally forced herself to speak after Adela asked if she was still there.

"Yes, I'm here. Ah . . . did Cabe happen to mention when he would be back?"

"No, dear. He was gone before I was up this morning."

Adela was mistaken, Summer thought. She had to be. "How do you know he's gone? Perhaps he only went out for a walk." For over eight hours? she asked herself. Don't be a ninny. You're grasping at straws, very flimsy straws.

Adela must have thought so too. "In the note he left, he said he was called back to Chicago and that he would let me know when he was going to return. He left a phone number where he could be reached in case of emergency. It's the number of someone named Star. That's all I know." After a short pause, she added, "I could give you the number if you need to get in touch with him."

"No," Summer said quickly. Closing her eyes, she managed to keep her voice steady as she lied through her teeth. "It's not important."

"I'm leaving for my sister's again around noon tomorrow and I'm taking Bailey with me. If Mr. Flynn phones before then, I will mention you called."

"That's not necessary." Desperately changing the subject, Summer asked, "How is your sister?"

In a martyred tone, Adela gave her opinion of her sister's household, including a vivid description of the noise and mess made by her nieces and nephews. The lengthy discourse gave Summer time to collect her scattered thoughts so that she could chat with Adela for a few more minutes before hanging up the phone.

Resting her elbows on the desk, she buried her face in her hands. The only sound was the rhythmic ticking of the clock in the outer office, but Summer didn't hear it. All she was aware of were the shattered dreams falling down around her.

Dropping her hands abruptly, she pushed her chair back and carefully, painstakingly checked her drawer to make sure it was locked, tested the door to the safe, and examined the catches on the windows. She yanked the paging unit off her belt and set it on top of the file cabinet. Then she shut the door, secured the outer office, and stepped outside.

On the top step, she looked out toward the island silhouetted against the sky. She thought of going there, then dismissed it. Even the magic of the island wouldn't soothe her tonight. She was more tempted to go home and crawl into bed, to pull the covers over her head like a child who wanted to escape from an unpleasant chore or from something scary.

She was no child. Last night she had told Cabe she knew what she was doing, but now she wasn't so sure. She had naively thought making love with Cabe would mean something to him, a sign that he cared for her. She couldn't have been more wrong. Apparently he considered making love as no more than sexual exercise without any emotional involvement.

Descending the steps, she headed toward her cabin. Some lessons come hard in life, and she had just been handed a doozy. It was up to her how she was going to handle it, by being angry and bitter or by putting it on a shelf with the other things she wished she'd done differently.

As she let herself into her cabin, she was glad

Cabe had never been inside. The only memories she had to deal with here were the ones in her own mind. And they were vivid and painful. The facade she had used to cover her shock at hearing he was gone dropped away and she curled up into a ball on her bed.

On Monday she attacked the day with a vengeance, as if it were an enemy she had to defeat. Leaving the staff to carry on their normal activities, she took on the most physically demanding jobs she could come up with, from waxing water skis and the exterior of the fiberglass boats not rented out to raking the sand on the beach to free it of litter and anything that might cut bare feet. Along with getting a great amount of work done, the only other thing she accomplished was getting two blisters on the palms of each hand. Her thoughts of Cabe hadn't been exorcized at all. They were as strong and as confused as ever.

When the noonday sun forced her to go to the office for a cool drink, Theresa told her there had been two long-distance calls for her from Chicago. Her heart flip-flopped as hope reared its stubborn head.

"Did he leave a message or a number where I could call him back?"

Theresa shook her head. "It was a woman, and no, she didn't leave a message. She just said she would call back later."

Scowling, Summer wondered if it was the same woman who had called Cabe the night she had answered his phone. The woman named Star. The woman whose phone number Cabe had left with Adela. She went into the small bathroom and washed her hands before splashing water on her flushed face. As she dried her face and hands with a rough towel, she heard the phone ring and Theresa's friendly voice answering it. Then Theresa called to Summer through the closed door.

Still holding the damp towel, Summer opened the door and walked over to the counter, where Theresa handed her the phone.

"This is Summer Roberts.

She recognized Star's voice, whose tone implied it was about damn time. "Cabe Flynn asked me to call to tell you he had to return to Chicago due to an emergency. He doesn't know when he will be able to phone you himself. Is there any message you want me to give him?"

"Yes," Summer said cooly. "Tell him not to worry. I got the message when I'd learned he had left town."

Without waiting to hear whatever else Star from Chicago might say, she handed the phone back to Theresa.

Ignoring the other woman's curious glance, she said, "I'll be in the boathouse." She pushed open the door, smiling politely at an older couple who were coming in.

Her smile disappeared as soon as she passed them. She couldn't believe it. He had the nerve to have his Chicago girlfriend call her with some hokey message. He didn't even have the courtesy to say good-bye in person. If that was how things were done in the big city, she thought it stank.

Summer realized the last page had been turned. The book of her love affair was short and sweet, but "The End" had been written, and it was time to put it away.

With renewed determination, she returned to her work.

Five days later Summer was exhausted. Her legs felt as though she had been on a treadmill, having walked forever without getting anywhere. She was working herself into the ground in an attempt to keep so busy she wouldn't think. As tired as she was at the end of the day, she found it difficult to sleep at night when it was quiet and thoughts of Cabe edged into her mind.

She turned down two invitations to have dinner with Celia and Harry, who were aware Cabe was no longer in town. Tact was not Celia's strongest point, and Summer knew she would ask questions Summer was not prepared to answer. Plus, Celia's sharp eyes could detect a gnat on a log at twenty paces. Cabe's rejection was too fresh for Summer to hide it from her friend.

In a tiny corner of her mind, the hope that Cabe might phone after all still valiantly held on by fragile fingers, but by the end of the week its grip had lost strength.

When the phone rang in the office before it was officially opened Saturday morning, Summer automatically answered it. Unable to sleep, she had come to the office to put the time to good use rather than waste it by staring at the ceiling in her bedroom.

Thinking it was either a wrong number or an early-bird tourist, she politely answered, "Roberts' Marina."

"Summer Roberts please."

Even though she had only heard the woman's voice twice before, Summer knew immediately who was on the other end of the line.

"Speaking."

"Miss Roberts, Cabe Flynn will be arriving at the Clearview Airport on a chartered flight, which should land around ten o'clock this morning. He has asked that you be there to pick him up."

"Really? Why would I do that?"

The woman paused, clearly surprised at Summer's response. "Because he asked you to. He needs your help."

"Look, Star, or whatever your name is. Cabe didn't need my help when he left. Why would he need my help coming back."

"Star? I think you've gotten a few things confused, Miss Roberts. I'm not Star. I'm Mr. Star's secretary."

"Who—who is Mr. Star?"

"Reese Star. Owner of Star Electronics. The man responsible for calling Cabe back to Chicago." The woman spoke impatiently. "Star would have called you himself, but he's taking Cabe to the airport. He's going to stay with Cabe and then fly back after he turns him over to you."

Summer didn't like the way that sounded, as if Cabe were a package. "Has something happened to Cabe? Is he all right?"

"Star will fill you in when he gets there." She gave Summer the name of the chartered airline and repeated the time of arrival. "Will you be there, Miss Roberts? If not, I'll have to make other arrangements to have Cabe transported to his house."

Fear stabbed through her, piercing the animosity she had wrapped around her the instant she heard the woman's voice. "I'll be there."

"Fine." The woman's voice changed, a shade warmer than before. "This isn't part of the message Star asked me to pass on, Miss Roberts, but if there is anything I can do, all you have to do is ask." She gave Summer a phone number, then added, "I mean it, Miss Roberts. Cabe paid a high price for saving Star Electronics, and we are all deeply grateful."

In a daze, Summer copied down the number and hung up the phone after the line went dead. Dead. That was how she would feel if anything happened to Cabe. Something was wrong, something serious, or he would have been able to fly back alone, without help.

She glanced up at the large clock on the wall. How was she going to get through the next four hours? She began pacing back and forth, going over every word the secretary had said, piecing together as much as she could with the information she had been given. Cabe's physical condition overruled the relief of finding out that the woman who had been phoning was the secretary of his friend and not . . . something else. The woman hadn't come right out and said Cabe was hurt, but the way she phrased things gave Summer the impression he was unable to manage on his own.

By the time her staff began arriving, she had imagined a variety of things wrong with him, from two broken legs to beriberi. It was impossible even to think of trying to work, so she decided to go back to her cabin. Before leaving, she phoned Adela to tell her to expect Cabe, but there was no answer. Then she remembered the housekeeper had taken advantage of his absence by visiting her sister. Whether she was there or not, though, his room would be ready.

Summer was at the Twin Cities airport a good hour before Cabe's flight was due in. There was nothing to do except wait, but she felt better being there than back at the marina. After asking where charter flights landed, she was directed to an area separate from the commercial airlines terminal. Her only companion in the small, nicely decorated waiting room was an older man in a dark business suit who kept his briefcase practically glued to his side. Since he was preoccupied with glancing at his watch every few seconds and staring out at an empty runway, he completely ignored her. That was fine with her. She wasn't in the mood to make polite conversation with a stranger anyway.

Before leaving for the airport, she had changed her clothes, more for something to do than from worrying about how she looked. The safari-style white shirt tucked into a pair of khaki slacks were more appropriate than her usual attire of shorts and T-shirt. She caught her reflection in the glass covering a print on the wall and saw a woman with anticipation mixed with fear in her eyes. As anxious as she was to see Cabe, she was uneasy about the strange way he was returning.

Finally, a Lear jet arrived, staying only long enough to collect the impatient man and his briefcase. As the jet taxied down the runway for takeoff into the wide blue yonder, she resumed the invisible path the businessman had taken.

Her pacing accelerated when ten o'clock came and went without any sign of a plane from Chicago. She found herself copying the businessman's habit of looking at her watch every few seconds.

When she was about ready to give up, a small jet landed and coasted up to the gate. The first man who stepped down was the epitome of the tall, dark, and handsome stranger. Thinking it was the wrong plane again, she started to turn away, when she saw another man help Cabe down the steps.

For a few seconds she was too shocked to move or even breathe as she watched the other man put one arm around Cabe's waist to support him. In his opposite hand he carried a suitcase. Cabe held his left arm across his waist and his right arm was over the other man's shoulder.

She ran out of the waiting room and through the gate. Without saying a word, she came up to Cabe's left side to help support him. He gave her a faint smile, acknowledging her presence, but he didn't seem to have the strength to talk. Their walk to the gate should have taken only a few minutes, yet it took over fifteen.

Inside, they led Cabe to one of the chairs, and he sat down heavily, still holding his side. Summer met the concerned gaze of the other man.

Extending her right hand, she said, "I'm Summer Roberts."

He shook her hand. "Hi. I'm Reese Star."

She nodded. "My Jeep is parked some distance away. It will take me about five minutes to bring it to the curb out front."

Reese Star nodded and watched as she turned and walked away. Sitting down beside Cabe, he said, "She doesn't rattle easy. She didn't ask a single question."

"She will," Cabe murmured in a strained voice.

"Do you still want me to leave right away? How the hell are you going to manage on your own?"

"We've been over this, Reese. I needed to get back here. I've left a lot of unfinished business that can't wait."

Reese chuckled. "I think I just met some of that business." His tone changed. He was no longer amused. "I heard the doctor tell you it was too soon for you to leave the hospital, Cabe. I hope to hell you know what you're doing."

"Just get me into her Jeep, and I'll take it from there."

Reese stood and helped Cabe to his feet. "Okay, macho dummy. Let's see you make it to the Jeep first."

Cabe made it. It took most of what little strength he had left, but he made it. After Cabe was settled in the front seat, Reese took Summer's arm and led her a little distance away.

He handed her a card. "This is my business card. I wrote my home number on the back. If you need me for anything, I want you to promise to call me."

"How bad are his injuries?" she asked. "I would ask him, but I don't think he would tell me."

There was respect in Reese's eyes as he looked down at her. "I see you know Cabe pretty well. Did he tell you anything about the work he's been doing for me?"

She shook her head.

"Now, why doesn't that surprise me?" he said with resignation. "I won't go into the details except to say he was finishing up a touchy investigation, and it was more dangerous than any of us expected." He waited to see how she took that bit of information before he went any further. She calmly gazed back at him.

"He has a knife wound in his side," he said bluntly.

She flinched only slightly. "He should be in a hospital, shouldn't he?"

Reese nodded. "But he basically needs to rest and let his wound heal. I suppose he can do that as easily in his home as in a hospital. Luckily, the knife was deflected by one of his ribs so his lung wasn't damaged, but he lost a lot of blood." He withdrew a small container from his jacket pocket. "This is the pain medication he was given when he left the hospital. The instructions are on the label."

"Summer!"

The hoarse, impatient shout came from her Jeep. She took the medication and put it into one of the pockets of her slacks. "I'll take care of him, Mr. Star."

He fell into step beside her as she started back toward the Jeep. "Call me Reese. And I know you will, Summer, or I wouldn't leave him here. I admit I thought he was crazy when he said he wanted to go home, but now I agree this is where he should be."

Summer wondered if *home* was the word Cabe had actually used or whether Reese had supplied the expression himself.

She got behind the steering wheel and retrieved a pad and pen from the glove compartment. She wrote down the number of the marina and handed it to Cabe's friend.

"Your secretary has the number, but in case she misplaced it, I want you to have it. I'm going to take Cabe to my cabin, and I don't have a phone, but during the day you can reach me at this number or leave a message."

"Why not take him to his grandfather's house?"

"The bedrooms are all on the second floor."

Reese nodded in understanding. Glancing over at Cabe, he saw he was scowling at them. He walked around to the other side of the Jeep to say good-bye to him. "Try to be a better patient for Summer than you were at the hospital. I've told her to give me a call if you or she need anything." To Summer, he grinned and said, "Good luck."

Cabe had both arms crossed over his waist, his mouth a tight white line as he attempted a smile. "I'll be fine."

With one last look at Summer, Reese nodded and walked back to the terminal.

Summer felt a moment of panic when Reese disappeared from view. The responsibility for Cabe was now hers alone. What she knew about caring for an injured person could be put into a thimble, and there would still be room left over. She shifted her gaze to Cabe. He didn't seem to share her concern. His eyes were closed as he leaned his head back on the seat. Either he trusted her completely or he had passed out.

She took extra pains to drive as carefully as she could so that she didn't jar him too much. Apparently she was successful, because his eyes remained closed and he didn't say a word. It took twice as long as it should have to reach her cabin, and several times drivers behind her were impatient with her slow speed. She ignored their honking horns and dirty looks.

Finally she turned onto her driveway and parked as close to the cabin as she could. When she shut the engine off, Cabe opened his eyes and started to get out of the Jeep on his own. She hurried around to him to prop her shoulder under his arm. As she slipped her arm around him, she could feel the heavy bandage wrapped in a wide swathe about his middle.

His breathing was shallow and obviously painful as he stepped up onto the first step. Walking the short distance from the Jeep had already taken a toll on his stamina.

"Lean on me, Cabe."

"I'm too heavy."

"I'm stronger than I look." She didn't know exactly where his injury was, so she didn't want to hold him anywhere near his ribs. Her hand closed over his opposite hip for leverage as he struggled up the next step.

Three steps later, Cabe's forehead was dotted with the sweat of exertion and he was gulping for air. With each step, he had slumped against her more and more until she was almost collapsing under his weight. His hand gripped the frame of the door and he paused for a moment.

Summer didn't ask him if he could make it any farther. He knew she couldn't get him into her bedroom alone, so all she could do was to wait until he felt he could go on.

They were both exhausted by the time they reached her bedroom. Cabe sank down heavily on the mattress and just sat there, unable to find the energy to lie down. Summer pulled back the covers, then knelt in front of him to unbutton his shirt.

He rested his arms heavily on her shoulders.

"At any other time I would enjoy having you take my clothes off."

She slid his shirt off and gently pressed against his bare shoulders to force him to lie back. Now she could see the white bandage covering most of his midsection, but because he was watching her, she kept her expression blank. She removed his shoes and socks, then sat on the bed to unfasten his slacks.

When her fingers slipped under his waistband, she heard his sharp intake of breath and raised her eyes to meet his. "Am I hurting you?"

A corner of his mouth curved up. "Yes, but not the way you mean."

Her eyes locked with his for a long moment. It was incredible, she thought. As badly as he felt, his eyes were warm with desire. She shook her head in amazement and exasperation. "I'm trying to make you as comfortable as I can, Cabe."

"Taking my pants off isn't the way to do it. Leave them for now. I have enough aches without adding one more."

She started to get off the bed, but he placed his hand on her thigh to stop her. "Don't go yet."

"Cabe, you need to rest."

"I will in a minute." He attempted to take a deep breath, but it hurt too much. He cut it off quickly. "I want to explain why I left so abruptly without calling you. I—"

She pressed her fingertips against his lips. "It doesn't matter now. What matters is that you get well. Everything else can wait until then."

He gave her a faint smile, his eyes heavy with weariness. "But we need to talk."

Her fingers were cool against his heated skin. "Try to sleep, Cabe. I'll be here when you wake up."

Her last words were the reassurance he needed,

and he gave in to the shuddering exhaustion and pain, finally willing to let his body have what it was crying out for so badly.

When she could feel his hand relax on her leg, Summer slipped out from under it and got off the bed. Looking down at him, she shoved her hands into her pockets, and her fingers closed around the small plastic vial Reese had given her. What a wonderful nurse she was, she groaned inwardly. She could have made him more comfortable by giving him his medication, but she had forgotten all about it. Taking it out of her pocket, she set it on the bedside table as a reminder for when he woke up.

After covering him with a quilt, she was at a loss as to what else to do for him. She pulled a rocking chair from the corner of her room until it was beside the bed. Then she sat down, her gaze remaining on Cabe's face.

Eight

Two hours later, Cabe hadn't moved. Neither had Summer. She stopped rocking and laid her hand on his forehead, and was relieved to feel his skin cool against her fingers.

He didn't react at all to her touch.

Since he seemed to be sleeping naturally without any sign of a fever, she decided to leave him for a few minutes. After one last look, she ran out the front door.

During the rest of the day, she spent a lot of time dashing back and forth from her cabin to the marina, then back again to check on Cabe. On one of her trips, she brought in his suitcase and left it in her bedroom on top of a trunk against a wall.

For the first time since taking over the marina, she asked Theresa to close up for her, and open in the morning too. She handed over the keys without a second thought and really couldn't blame the woman for looking at her as though she had lost her mind. In the three years Theresa had worked for Summer, no one had ever opened or closed or run the marina but the boss.

Going back through the hedge, Summer forget entirely about the marina, which would have surprised her if she had stopped to think about it. The marina had been the most important thing in her life, but she had simply turned her back on it in order to take care of Cabe.

When she looked in on him, he was still asleep, yet was becoming restless. He had kicked off the quilt and was partially lying on his right side, his hand protecting his left ribs. She went into the kitchen to prepare him something to eat. He had slept through lunch and was bound to be hungry when he woke up. Her cupboards weren't exactly full, but she did find a can of vegetable-beef soup.

He was awake when she carried the tray containing a bowl of soup into the bedroom. "Hi. Are you hungry?"

He nodded and attempted to sit up. His face contorted in a painful grimace, and he stopped trying, falling back onto the mattress. She placed the tray on her dresser and sat down beside him.

"Where is the wound?"

"Left side."

She was on his right side. "Take my arm and pull yourself up. I'll put another pillow behind you."

The simple act of sitting up caused a light sheen of perspiration to break out on his forehead. After she'd eased him down onto the pillows, she started to stand, but he rested his hand on her thigh. His glance roamed around the room and then back to her. "This is your bedroom, isn't it?"

She nodded. "I thought you would prefer tackling the five steps outside to the long stairway at Hadley's. Besides, Adela doesn't answer, so she must still be at her sister's. You wouldn't have anyone to take care of you if I took you to your grandfather's house."

"This isn't what I had in mind when I told Reese to get me back here," he said, a hint of apology in his voice. "I didn't plan on turning you into a nurse."

"That's good because I'm not very good at it." She smiled at him. "If you were a boat, I would know what to do to make you work better, but when it comes to knife wounds, I'm at a complete loss."

Anger flashed in his eyes, then it was gone. "Reese has a big mouth."

"If he hadn't told me, I would have asked. It was obvious something was wrong when I saw you get out of the plane." She changed the subject and slid off the bed. "I heated up some soup for you."

Cabe obediently ate the soup and took the two pills she gave him without any protest. To his mind, he was causing Summer enough trouble. Reese had been right. He really hadn't been up to making the trip to Clearview. Yet when he had heard her response to his message through Reese's secretary, he had known Summer had put the wrong meaning to his abrupt departure the morning after he had made love to her. It was important to clear up the misunderstanding between them as soon as possible.

But it would have to wait. The combination of his injury, the trip from Chicago, and the medication made it impossible for him to stay awake. He had to be content with feeling her hand in his as he drifted off to sleep.

During the night he woke to a nearly dark room. His sleep-fogged brain cleared, and he realized where he was. He didn't need a light to see who was beside him in the bed. Summer's warm body was pressed against his right side, her soft hair spread over the pillow near his head.

Moonlight was shining faintly into the room through the single window, enough for him to see the doorway leading, he hoped, to a bathroom. All he had to do was get there. Hoping he wouldn't disturb Summer, he pushed himself up and stood shakily on his feet, his right hand holding his left side. He stayed motionless while the room spun ominously. It finally righted itself, and he felt he could make it to the bathroom without falling flat on his face.

He shut the bathroom door first before turning on the light, and a few minutes later, flicked off the light before opening the door. His attempt to keep from waking Summer had been futile, though. The lamp on the beside table was on, and Summer was standing near the bathroom door.

Even though his side burned as if someone had laid a red-hot poker against it, he couldn't help smiling.

She looked like a pouty child awakened abruptly from her nap. Her hair was mussed and her eyes were half-closed as she stood in front of him wearing a white Victorian nightgown that flowed down to the floor. His smile widened as she plodded along beside him back to the bed, neither taking his arm nor saying a thing. She didn't seem to notice he had removed his slacks while he was in the bathroom and was wearing only his briefs. She waited until he was lying back down, then stumbled around the foot of the bed to the other side. She switched off the lamp and slipped under the covers, then seemed to immediately fall asleep, her hand resting possessively on his arm.

He gently slipped his right arm under her and brought her over toward him. Her head fell easily on his shoulder and remained there. Still smiling, Cabe closed his eyes.

The tantalizing smell of fresh coffee nudged him awake the next morning. One glance at the space beside him showed him he was alone, and the familiar sounds of cooking told him where Summer was.

Fifteen minutes later he left the bedroom, dressed in his slacks and shirt, although he hadn't bothered to button the latter. He had taken the time to shave, and that had made him feel more human, but he would have traded his car to be able to take a shower. He walked through the living room to the kitchen, pausing for a moment to admire the cheerful decor of her home. At the kitchen door he stopped and smiled at the long length of her legs exposed by the short robe she had put on after her shower. Damp tendrils of hair clung to her cheek as the rest of her hair flowed down her back in gentle waves.

She was setting the tray and dropped a spoon onto the floor when he suddenly spoke behind her.

"You won't need the tray, Summer. I'll eat breakfast out here with you."

She whirled around. "Cabe, are you crazy. You shouldn't be out of bed."

"I've been in bed for the last four days. Humor me for a little while." He pulled out a chair and sat down at the table, his hand spread across his middle as before.

She brought him a cup of coffee, then turned back to the stove to crack several eggs into a frying pan. "If you fall off that chair, Cabe Flynn, I'm going to leave you lying on the floor."

For the first time in days, Cabe laughed. It hurt

like hell but, he couldn't help it. She was so ador-
ably grumpy.

Summer shook her head in exasperation. As
she cracked another egg into a skillet, she was
smiling. She felt lighter than she had since she
had first seen him getting off the plane. If he
could laugh, he was well on the way to recovery.
The tight coil of tension eased in her chest. He
was going to be all right.

She prepared a huge breakfast of eggs, bacon,
juice, and biscuits and placed a large glass of milk
in front of him. Considering all he had been
through, it wasn't surprising he wasn't able to eat
everything she had piled on his plate. Sitting across
from him, she could see he was beginning to tire,
but he did manage to put away enough to satisfy
her.

He eyed the glass of milk suspiciously. "What
am I supposed to do with that?"

"Usually people drink it."

"I hate milk."

"It's good for you. It's supposed to build strong
bones and stuff like that."

"Summer, I'm not nine. I outgrew milk years
ago." He glanced at the kitchen clock on the wall
behind her. "You're going to be late opening up
the marina. It's almost eight o'clock."

"'I'm not going to the marina today. Theresa is
going to be in charge. Now, don't try to change
the subject. Drink your milk."

There were golden lights of amusement in his
eyes as he lifted the glass, giving her a mock
salute before drinking it all in one go.

"Satisfied?"

"Yes. Don't you feel better?"

"Gobs. Why aren't you going to the marina?"

She pushed her chair back and began to clear
the table. "I decided to take the day off."

Her casual reply shook him. "You don't have to do that, Summer. I don't need a baby-sitter. I'll probably spend the day in bed."

Steadying himself by placing his right hand on the table, he stood up. Damned if the floor didn't start bobbing up and down like the surface of the lake.

Summer had dumped their dishes into the sink and was turning back to the table when she saw him waver. Moving quickly to his side, she put her arm around him. "Sit down before you fall down."

He shook his head. Draping his arm over her shoulders, he murmured, "I'll be all right in a minute."

She turned him in the direction of her bedroom and began walking, forcing him to go with her. "I thought Hadley was the most stubborn man I had ever met, but you've got him beat."

When they reached her bed, he sank down gratefully onto it. He laid back and held his side as he took short, gasping breaths. "I guess I'm not as chipper as I thought I was."

She lifted his feet onto the bed and was going to leave him so that he could rest, but he called her back. "Summer?"

"Do you want your medication?"

He shook his head. "Take off my slacks."

It wasn't so much what he said as the way he was looking at her that made her bones turn to jelly. She did as he asked as efficiently as possible, folding his slacks over the back of a chair. She started for the door again, but again he called her back.

"Summer?"

Scowling, she turned. "What?"

"Come here." He patted the mattress beside him,

shifting his hips over so that she had room. "I want to talk to you."

When she hesitated, he said wearily, "Don't make me get up and come after you."

She slowly returned to the bed. "We can talk later, Cabe. You need to rest."

"I am resting, dammit," he said heatedly. He raised up to grab her hand and pull her down onto the bed. The bouncing of the mattress and the exertion of tugging at her hand was too much. His side instantly complained about the abuse, and he flinched, biting back a groan.

Feeling responsible for his pain because she hadn't done as he asked before, she sat down, holding his hand tightly, waiting for him to say whatever he felt was so important to say.

Gradually his fingers loosened their grip on hers, and he could breathe more evenly. "Summer, when I left you that night, there was a message waiting for me to call Reese no matter what time I got back. The investigation I had started before I left Chicago was breaking open. I had to leave right away, or everything we had worked for would be useless. Reese could have lost everything he had if we didn't catch the person who was stealing the plans for several top-secret projects his company was developing for the government.

"What happened?"

"I caught her," he said flatly.

"Her?"

The surprise in her voice made him smile. "I believe that is a reverse sexist remark, Summer. Women have been known to steal too."

"I know. But you were . . ." Her gaze shifted to his bandaged side.

"Women have been known to knife people too." There was a calm acceptance in his voice that drew her eyes to his. What kind of life had he led that he could appear so cool about being stabbed? she wondered. Apparently he considered it a common occurrence to put himself into a position where he could be hurt.

Her eyes glistened with unshed tears. "My God, Cabe. It doesn't matter whether the person who held the knife was a man or a woman. You could have been killed."

He slowly raised his hand to touch the tear falling down her cheek. "Why are you crying?" he asked. His voice was full of wonder.

She refused to look away. "I'm not crying."

The back of his finger caught another tear. "If you're not crying, then what is this?"

She rubbed her hand roughly across her cheek. "I'm angry."

He continued to caress her damp cheek with his knuckle. "Why?"

"Because you are so incredibly stupid."

"Am I? And that makes you cry?"

Her voice cracked. "I'm not crying. I never cry."

His hand moved to her shoulder and drew her down to lie beside him. He rolled onto his side, ignoring the searing pain. It was inconsequential compared with the agony he saw in her face.

"Summer, I'm trying my damndest to be honest with you. I know you put the wrong meaning to my leaving Clearview after we made love, but I've explained that. It's your turn to be honest with me. Tell me why you're so angry."

"Because you go willingly into situations where you could be hurt."

He stared at her, stunned into silence. She was implying more than the fear of his being harmed physically. She was angry because it mattered. She cared, and it wasn't easy for her.

When she put pressure against his arms, he thought she was trying to move off the bed. Instead, she was only changing position to lie on her back next to him. His arm was resting across her waist, and she didn't make any attempt to remove it. Her tears had stopped, but her eyes were incredibly sad as she stared up at the ceiling.

Instinctively he knew she was fighting an inner battle with herself. He could only wait to see if he was the winner, or if the years of hiding her feelings would continue to be her defense.

There was an odd detachment in her voice as her gaze remained fixed on the ceiling. "There are forty-seven boards and twelve knotholes up there. I've counted them. Over and over again I've counted them like someone who can't sleep counts sheep. But it never helped. You wouldn't go away."

Cabe stiffened and slowly raised himself on his arm, completely oblivious of the twinge of pulled stitches as he looked down at her.

Still she stared at the ceiling. "For over ten years you've been here. I visualized the white bandage on your shoulder when Hadley told me you had been shot. I saw you in your black dinner jacket with that blond actress on your arm, the one you escorted to the theater one night when Hadley was visiting you. Everything Hadley told me about you I would picture in my mind when I came back home. It doesn't seem at all odd that you're here now. You've been a guest in this room since I was sixteen."

She turned her head enough to be able to see his face. Already pale, he now looked like a man in shock. "You've been like the carousel. An illusion, something to think about, to dream about, to escape with in my mind, to ride off into the sunset with toward an imaginary world where there are no problems, no pain, no mundane daily hassles of worrying about money and responsibilities." She laughed self-consciously. "That's something for a grown woman to admit, isn't it? There's supposed to be a time when we put aside the belief in fairy tales and fantasies."

"Everyone has fantasies, no matter how old he or she is. The only difference is that grown-ups are supposed to know which is real and which is imaginary."

"Have you ever had any fantasies?" she asked curiously.

The corners of his eyes crinkled with amusement. "I've had my share. When I was around fifteen, I had a terrific fantasy about Jill Marshall. She was a cheerleader and a senior, way too old for me, but she had two sensational . . . ah, pom-poms."

"I think that's called lust, not fantasy," Summer said dryly.

"I grew up in an atmosphere of fantasy, remember? Hadley liked to create a playland where people of all ages could lose themselves for a while in the land of make-believe and fun. Some of my playmates were jugglers, trapeze artists, and clowns who would come to visit Hadley. Many of them lived out a lot of people's dreams of running away to a circus." He stroked the soft skin of her throat. "There's nothing wrong with a good old fantasy, Tinkerbell. We all need them occasionally."

She studied him carefully, beginning to believe he understood. "That's why I don't want to lose the carousel."

"What about losing me?' he asked quietly.

She frowned. "I can't lose what I don't have."

"I'm not an illusion or a fantasy, Summer. I'm very real, and I'm not going anywhere." He picked up a long strand of her hair and watched it curl around his finger. It reminded him of how she had wound her way around his heart. "You don't have to look up at the ceiling to find me. I'll be right beside you."

"You don't have to say that, Cabe," she said flatly as she sat up and swung her legs over the side of the bed.

"I think you need to hear it."

Glancing over her shoulder, she met his serious gaze. "We both know you will be here only until you clear up Hadley's estate and your injury heals."

She slid off the bed. Cabe grabbed her hand to stop her, but had forgotten about his stitches. A blunt curse followed a sharp intake of air, and he fell back against the pillow, still holding onto her hand.

In an attempt to break her fall, she flung out her arm to the other side of his hips to keep from landing on his injured side.

"What are you trying to do?" she scolded. "I could have hurt you."

He positioned her so that she was partially lying on top of him on his right side. "I'm trying to keep you from leaving," he said roughly. "You have a nasty habit of walking out on conversations just when they start getting interesting."

To enable her to see his face better, she shifted a little against him, her hip against his. "I do not."

His hand slid to the small of her back to keep her still. "If you don't stop squirming, we're going to be having more than a conversation."

When it dawned on her what he meant, she froze in his arms. Then a glint of mischief brightened her smile. "I don't think you're quite up to anything but conversation at the moment."

The look in his eyes was blatantly sensual as his hands clamped down on her hips, moving her lower body over his thighs. He saw her eyes change from a tranquil green sea to stormy turbulence when he pressed her into his aroused body. "You were saying?"

"Cabe," she murmured huskily. "This is insane. You'll rip open your stitches."

He cursed the woman who had inflicted the damn stab wound. He knew Summer was right, but he didn't have to like it. "I'll settle for a kiss for now."

Her breath caught in her throat as he brought her head down and kissed her with a demanding hunger that belied his physical condition. His tongue took the liberties his body couldn't take at the moment, thrusting into the warm intimacy of her soft mouth as his hands ground her into his hips.

Holding herself away from his injured side with one hand on the mattress, she took what he offered, giving him the freedom to do as he liked with her mouth.

A warm hand slid between the opening of her robe and covered her breast. A groan of need was absorbed between them, neither sure who made the sound and not really caring.

A point was reached when their bodies cried out for more than was possible under the circumstances. Cabe reluctantly released his caressing hold on her breast and with a deep sigh lowered her head to his shoulder. He held her for a long time while their pulses slowed. The flames of passion were allowed to cool, but remained like banked live coals, needing only a small amount of fanning to spring to life again.

Cabe's breathing was less ragged, but Summer knew he was taking short breaths because it hurt him to breathe normally. Raising her head, she looked down at him. Pain had dulled his eyes and tightened his mouth.

This time he didn't resist when she sat up to examine his bandage. She sighed with relief when she saw it was still spotlessly white. "No harm seems to be done." She lifted her gaze to meet his, and her voice held a hint of pleading. "Will you rest now, please?"

"I don't seem to have a choice."

She brought him a glass of water from the bathroom, then lifted his head so that he could take his pills and drink from the glass. She pulled the sheet up to cover him to the waist. "I'm going to run over to the marina to make sure Theresa isn't having any problems and I'll be back."

He nodded and closed his eyes.

She looked in on him several times during the day, waking him at noon to eat lunch. He went back to sleep almost as soon as she had taken his tray away.

By evening, he had had all the sleep he needed and came out to the table to eat dinner. She didn't insist he eat in bed. Not that it would do any good anyway, she thought. Only he could judge how he felt.

While he ate, she told him Reese had phoned to ask how he was doing.

"And what did you say?"

"I told him you were resting. Oh, he said to tell you the district attorney is going to prosecute the computer operator on the evidence you provided."

He nodded as though it were what he expected and went on to something that he had been curious about. "Why don't you have a phone, Summer?"

"I never needed one here. I usually spend most of my time at the marina."

"And you don't have a television for the same reason?"

"I don't spend much time here except to sleep."

That was an accurate description of the use he made of his own apartment in Chicago. He did have a telephone and a television, but he rarely used either one.

"You obviously spend some time in the kitchen," he said. "You're a good cook."

She smiled as he helped himself to more food. "I'm not that good a cook. Anyone can make spaghetti."

"I can't."

"You don't cook for yourself at all?"

He munched on another piece of garlic bread. "I can, but I don't bother. When I first moved to Chicago, I was a whiz with frozen dinners, but I couldn't take a steady diet of plastic food. I eat out most of the time."

And not alone either, she would wager. "I might as well admit it, I didn't cook tonight. I stopped by the restaurant and had the cook fix us some takeout."

His fork paused midway to his mouth. "I forgot about the restaurant." Setting his fork down, he leaned his forearms on the table. "You've made a lot of changes over the years. A restaurant, a gift shop. Another boathouse. What's next?"

She pushed her chair back and began gathering her plate and silverware. "It depends."

"On what?"

"On whether or not I get the loan to pay you the money for the island." She turned on the faucet to fill the sink with water. "If I get the loan, I won't be expanding any further. If I don't get the loan, I'll probably add more boats and update the ones I have."

Cabe had suddenly lost his appetite. Good Lord, he thought. She was serious. She was willing to mortgage the rest of her life for a chunk of land and a carousel.

With everything that had been happening, he had forgotten about the island and the week she had asked for. She hadn't. At the time, he had given her the week because it was a way of blackmailing her into using his name, but she had seriously wanted that time.

When she returned to the table, he pushed his plate away. "Are you finished?" she asked.

He nodded and watched her as she continued to clear the table. He wanted to tell her to forget the loan. She could have the whole island, the carousel, and anything else she wanted, but he doubted if she would accept it if he just handed it over to her. He would have to find some way to clear up the situation with the island and get it out of their way.

There were a lot of things he needed to clear up, and soon.

She was drying her hands when he stood up stiffly. He walked through the living room toward the front door instead of the bedroom. "Where are you going?" she asked.

"I'm getting cabin fever. I'm going for a walk." He opened the screen door and looked back at her. "Are you coming?"

Now she knew what Reese meant when he had wished her good look. Cabe was not acting like her idea of someone who was recovering from a stabbing. She shrugged. She wasn't exactly her idea of a first-class nurse either.

Once out on the porch, Cabe decided not to try the steps after all. He attempted to sit on the swing, but that simple act caused him more pain than he expected.

Summer stood in the doorway watching him

wrestle with the swing. When he finally gave up, she held the door open for him.

"I know, I know," he said. "I need to go back to bed."

"I didn't say anything."

"Your eyes did and very loudly." He released a martyred sigh. "I hate to admit it, but you and your eyes are right."

He draped his arm around her shoulders and accompanied her back into the cabin.

Nine

During the next couple of days, they shared the cabin, meals, and a bed. Cabe spent most of the time resting, and Summer spent more time at the marina. It was an unusual feeling for her to return home and have someone waiting for her.

And he was always waiting.

As each day went by, Cabe became more impatient. He thought he should be able to do more than he was, and it was driving him crazy. Having Summer's warm body next to him every night wasn't doing much for his sanity either. When she was there, he stayed in a perpetual state of wanting her. When she wasn't there, it was even worse.

On the third day, they had a brief but colorful debate before Summer left for the marina. He had wanted to come, too, but she asked him to rest one more day, finally convincing him it was for his own good. Or she thought she had convinced him.

Cabe was bored silly.

When she came home to see him around lunchtime, she brought him the magazines he had asked for earlier that morning. Around two o'clock, she returned and handed him the deck of cards he wanted. At four o'clock, he was sitting on the porch swing throwing the cards into an empty flowerpot. He wasn't at all happy when she said she was returning to the marina instead of staying home as she had been doing previously.

As she walked through the hedge, she looked back and saw he was still sitting in the swing. He looked as dejected as a little boy who hadn't been invited to a party that everyone else was going to. Suddenly she smiled and hurried back to the marina. Twenty minutes later she returned, squirming through the opening in the hedge carrying two bulging sacks in her arms.

Cabe had moved inside and was sprawled out on the bed, staring at the ceiling with one arm under his head. Surprised to see her so soon, he asked, "What's going on?"

"You want something to do, don't you? Well . . ." She dumped the contents of the sacks onto the bed. "Here's some things to play with."

Cabe began to smile as he examined every single item she had bought. There was a coloring book, a box of crayons, another deck of cards, a lump of clay, some puzzles, and even a small machine gun that shot bubbles into the air.

He started laughing. It hurt like hell, but he couldn't stop. Holding his side, he swept all the games and toys off the bed onto the floor, then tugged at her hand, tumbling her down beside him.

Still grinning, he rolled onto his good side to face her. "I get the picture. I'm acting like a child, right?"

She looked up in his dark eyes, tracing the laugh lines at the corners with her finger. "You're feeling better and you're bored. It's understandable, but all the gift shop had were things for children. Not that I know what men like to play with."

Moving his hand to the waistband of her shorts, he toyed with the front closure. "I'll show you," he said huskily. He unfastened the snap and lowered the zipper so that his hand could slide down over her belly.

"Cabe," she murmured. "You'll hurt yourself."

"I'm already hurting." His hand slipped lower. "I've been aching for you for days."

She closed her eyes as his fingers moved over her and in her, fanning the flames that had been kindling inside her. A soft whimper of need escaped her lips, and he kissed her. She should tell him to stop but, Lord, it felt so good. He felt so good. Her hands peeled away his shirt and glided over his strong muscles and heated skin. She gloried in his shudders of response. It still amazed her that she could make Cabe tremble with desire. The man she had dreamed about, had fantasized about, wanted her.

When he rolled on top of her, she saw him flinch as his injury protested. Surprising them both by taking the initiative, she gently pushed him over to lie on his back. Her expertise came from love, not experience, but it was more than enough. Her hands flowed over him, rubbing, caressing, stroking, as she lowered her head to taste and savor him.

Cabe was dying. Yet he had never felt more alive in his life. He swept away her clothing in a rush to have her naked skin against his. He had wanted her before, but never like this. Nothing had ever been like this. He was losing himself in her fragrance, her heat, her softness.

His control snapped when her small hand closed

over the most sensitive part of his body, the heat and silky feel of her fingers driving him to madness.

He raised his hips to meet her and heard her moan and felt her tremble against him. Her body gripped his tightly, and he thought he would explode from the myriad sensations slicing through him.

Together they were swept into a shimmering, hot, sensual whirlpool, drowning in each other as the ripples of need surged through them.

Gradually they fell back to earth. Even in her dazed state, Summer was aware of his bandaged side as she lay cradled in his arms. Afraid her weight was hurting him, she started to move off him, but he wouldn't let her go.

"No, stay." His voice was husky and low. "Just a little longer. I don't want to leave you yet."

She protested, but not very strongly. "I'm too heavy for you." She wanted to prolong the intimacy too.

"No, never." He tenderly brushed the tendrils of hair from the sides of her face. "We have some decisions to make, Summer. And soon."

She wasn't sure what he meant. "About what?"

"About Hadley's property, the present, the future." His forefinger smoothed over her full lower lip, his gaze on her moist mouth. Then he raised his eyes to meet hers. "And us."

"*We* have to make the decisions? Aren't those decisions for you to make alone?"

His gaze was serious and steady. "I'm no longer alone." His fingertips moved across her jaw, down her throat, and over her breasts. "I have you."

Her hips writhed against him, inciting and exciting him. "Yes, you do," she whispered as he arched his lower body into hers.

The incredible sequence was starting all over

again. "The decisions will have to wait," he murmured. "I can't."

When she closed her eyes as he moved against her, he said huskily, "Summer, look at me."

Slowly, she opened her eyes and met his dark gaze.

He arched his hips against her. "I love you."

She gasped as he surged into her with the same impact his words had on her. Her eyes closed as she fell into the oblivion of passion, unable to say the words he wanted to hear.

Later when she could find the breath to talk, she murmured against his throat, "I love you, too, Cabe. I have for a very long time."

Pulling her even closer, he marveled at how wonderful those simple words were to hear. "Loving you was one decision I didn't have to think about. It just happened."

Over the next couple of days, they spent every available moment together. Cabe was healing quickly and was able to do more as time passed. They had a picnic on the island. They watched the bathtub race from the shore. The race was an annual event in which the boats could be made of anything—milk cartons, orange crates, horse troughs—anything, but actual boats. Their evenings were spent in Summer's cabin or walking along the shore of the lake. One night they played backgammon, which Cabe preferred to his grandfather's game of chess.

During the whole time they were together, whatever they were doing, they talked. The little things became important. They exchanged their different and similar tastes in music, food, literature, their viewpoints on a variety of subjects, from politics to sports.

They stayed away from any discussion of the future of the island or their relationship. They lived for the moment, putting as much into each hour they were together as they could. Desire was always simmering between them and occasionally boiled over, always glorious and immediate.

The day Cabe had his stitches removed, he wanted to celebrate and asked her to go out to dinner that evening. Even though they had been virtually living together for a week, it was the first time they had actually had a "date." He took her Jeep and was gone all afternoon, returning dressed in a suit and tie to pick her up at seven. It had been a while since he had seen her wearing anything other than casual clothing, and when he walked in, he stopped abruptly.

Her cheeks flushed as he stared at her as though he had never seen her before. Feeling self-conscious in her high heels, with her hair arranged in an understated but elegant coil behind her head, she brushed an invisible wrinkle out of her teal-green and white floral skirt. Her white camisole top had thin straps that left her tanned shoulders bare and it hugged her breasts and waist.

"You're looking at me like you've never seen me before," she said defensively.

"I haven't. Not this Summer." He stepped closer and lifted his hand to her face, stroking the back of a knuckle over her soft golden skin. "There are so many Summers. I wonder if I'll ever get to know them all, to learn everything I want to know about you."

Nuzzling the palm of his hand, she looked down so that he couldn't see the pain in her eyes she was afraid she couldn't conceal. There wasn't going to be time for him to learn more about her. Soon he would be gone. She would grasp every minute with him she could and hope she could graciously let him go when it was time.

Applying a little pressure with his fingers under her chin, he brought her gaze up to meet his. What he saw in her eyes was a reflection of what was in his heart. The past week had been a hiatus of lovemaking and companionship, but nothing had really been settled. And he was running out of time.

Lifting his other hand, he held out a single yellow rose to her. "The first time I really saw you was at Hadley's funeral. There were a mass of flowers on his coffin, but I only remember the rose you held. Since then you've stood out in my mind like the rose stood out among all the other flowers."

He rarely gave her such compliments, and she melted under the softly spoken words.

A corner of his mouth curved up in a gentle smile. "Don't look at me like that, Summer, or we'll be late for our reservation."

"We don't have to go out at all," she said quietly, feeling the desire his touch always created.

"Yes, we do. It may seem a little backward to be wooing you with flowers and dinner at this point in our relationship, but I want to take you out."

As she went down the steps on his arm, she wondered if he was giving her a final evening with all the trimmings as a way of letting her down gently.

The following day Cabe asked her to drive him to Hadley's house before she went to the marina.

"You aren't planning to go through Hadley's possessions, are you? The doctor told you not to lift anything heavy for the next two weeks."

"I'm not going to move anything heavier than a telephone."

He leaned over and kissed her when she continued to frown at him. "I'll behave. I promise."

She dropped him off in front of the lovely old house. She nodded when he asked her to come back for him after she had closed the marina, then she drove away. Even though he was only going to be on the other side of the lake, she couldn't get rid of the feeling that there was a greater distance growing between them.

Everything ran smoothly at the marina, and there wasn't enough to keep her mind from returning to Cabe. At noon, she was tempted to take some lunch to him. Adela wouldn't be there to fix him anything, and there probably wasn't much in the house to eat, but something held her back. He had told her he loved her, and at the time the words had been enough. Now she needed to hear something about their future. Or did they even have one? she couldn't help wondering. Would he say, "I love you," as he got back on the plane for Chicago?

His absence from her life would be difficult enough to live with, but compounded with the dangers involved in his job, she would undoubtedly be old before her time, worrying about his welfare and never knowing if he was safe.

At three o'clock her musings were interrupted by a phone call from the developer who was interested in buying the island. After explaining who he was, he immediately got to the point.

"I've just received a phone call from Mr. Flynn, Miss Roberts. He informed me the island would not be for sale, but I was hoping to be able to persuade *you* to sell us *your* half of the island. Then we stand a good chance of changing Mr. Flynn's mind about his half of the property."

Speechless, Summer gripped the phone hard as the man continued to spout facts and figures his company had compiled. Feasibility studies, growth potential, and dollar figures were thrown at her, but she was only half-listening. Cabe had turned down the offer.

Thinking she was simply holding out for more money, the developer raised his bid, but Summer flatly refused it. The man on the other end of the phone would have been amazed to see how happy turning down an astonishing amount of money had made her. It was the easiest thing she had ever done. With a barely polite good-bye, she replaced the receiver.

Quickly punching in a number, she waited patiently for the bank's operator to answer. When she finally did, Summer asked to speak to Mr. Spaulding and was put on hold for a few minutes. She restlessly tapped the top of her desk as she waited, having no choice but to listen to the elevator music coming through the line.

Finally Richard answered. "Hello, Summer. How are you?"

"Fine, fine," she replied offhandedly. "Listen, Richard. I've changed my mind about the loan."

Relief was apparent in the older man's voice. "I was hoping you would. I haven't had much success getting any other financial institution to loan you as much as you needed without exorbitant interest. What changed your mind?"

"It's not necessary. Cabe no longer wants to sell the island."

"That's wonderful news. I heard he doesn't plan to sell Hadley's house either. Maybe he's decided to stay in Clearview after all."

This seemed to be a day for startling news. "Maybe," she answered abstractedly. "I really don't know what his plans are."

There was a buzzing sound in the background, then Richard said, "I have a call on another line, Summer. Thanks for calling me. You've made the right decision about the loan."

After she hung up, Summer sat behind her desk for a few minutes. Then she bolted out of her chair and strode out to the outer office.

She had to wait for Theresa to finish talking to a customer. When the man left, she asked, "Theresa, would you mind taking over the rest of the day? I know I've put a lot of extra work on you this past week, but I need to take care of something right away."

"No problem. I've enjoyed it. I'll call my husband, Jerry, if you don't mind. He's been coming in every day for a few hours. He especially enjoys talking to the tourists and helps answer the phone when it gets particularly busy." After a short pause, she added, "It's been very good for him. He's been at loose ends since he got laid off. I suppose I should have asked you first, though."

Shaking her head, Summer put her hand on Theresa's arm. "It's all right." She knew the older woman worried about her husband. He had been depressed ever since he lost his job. "Maybe we should put Jerry on the payroll."

Theresa looked genuinely surprised and pleased. "Do you mean it?"

"Talk it over with him and let me know how he feels about it. I'll see you later."

The drive to Hadley's house took the normal length of time, but Summer thought she would never get there. She had to know what Cabe had meant by refusing to sell the island and keeping Hadley's house.

She parked in the driveway and went through the side door. As she walked through the kitchen and dining room, her rubber-soled shoes made no sound on the polished wood floor. She could hear Cabe's voice coming from Hadley's study. She was going to go directly in, but when she had her hand on the partially opened door, she heard him say something about the carousel and stopped.

He gave details of the style, the age, the designer, and the location of the carousel. Then he said, "See if you can find out the approximate value of it, Reese. I could send photos if it will help, but that will take time, and I want to get this settled as quickly as possible."

Slowly Summer backed away from the door. When she ended up against the opposite wall of the hallway, she wrapped her arms around her middle. She felt light-headed and realized she had been holding her breath ever since she heard Cabe mention the carousel. She had to get out of there. He may have refused to sell the island, but he was about to dispose of the carousel. Her carousel.

She retraced her steps to the side door and quietly let herself out. She ran to her Jeep, released the brake, and coasted down the driveway before starting the engine.

She had no idea where she was going but it wasn't back to the marina or her cabin. She needed to get away, somewhere where she could think, try to make some sense of this whole thing.

There had to be a way to preserve the carousel. It was impossible to hide it or move it. He legally owned half of the island, and she didn't know if she could fight if he went ahead and sold whatever he wanted.

How could he even think of cold-bloodedly getting rid of the horses? she asked herself. He knew how important they were to her and had been to Hadley. Didn't sentiment mean anything to him? She thought she had gotten to know him as a sensitive, caring man. Evidently she had been wrong.

In a way it wasn't the disposal of the carousel itself that was bothering her. It had been unrealistic to think she would be able to keep it to herself forever anyway. She had toyed with the idea of rebuilding the amusement park someday so that the carousel would know the joy of children's laughter once again and could bring pleasure to everyone. But that was also unrealistic. She had neither the time, the money, nor the experience to take on the management of an amusement park. But there had to be some way to preserve the carousel. There had to be.

How could Cabe even think of selling it in the first place without discussing it with her? she asked herself over and over as she drove past the city limits of Clearview. Apparently she had been seeing him through love-tinted glasses and not seeing him clearly. The blinders were off now. She was going to lose him, the carousel, and her dreams.

Unless she did something about it.

Ten

By seven o'clock, Cabe was on the telephone calling around to try to find Summer. By eight o'clock he was pacing the floor, waiting for Richard Spaulding to arrive.

When the doorbell rang, he yanked open the door. "Was she at the marina?" he asked immediately.

Richard came in, shaking his head. "No, she wasn't there. The marina is closed, and no one is there, not even Jacob."

"Dammit, where can she be? She can't just disappear off the face of the earth. She has to be somewhere."

Richard looked closely at Cabe, then took his arm. "Let's go into the library," he suggested. "We'll sit down and think about this rationally."

A few minutes later Richard had poured them each a drink. "As I told you on the phone," he said as he sat down, "I heard from her earlier today when she told me she no longer needed the loan to buy the island. She said you didn't want to sell the island, so it wasn't necessary to borrow the money to buy you out."

Cabe frowned. "How in the hell did she know that? I called the developer only this morning."

"She didn't say."

"What about the woman who's been taking over the marina the past week? Theresa something or other. I don't know her last name, so I couldn't call her. She might know where Summer is."

Nodding, Richard told him the woman's name. Cabe leafed through the phone directory until he found her phone number. Then he waited and waited while the ringing sound droned on, as irritating and as incessant as a dentist's drill.

"No one answers." He crashed the receiver down. "Dammit, Richard. Where in hell is she?"

"I don't know, Cabe."

"What about Jacob? He might know something." Pulling the phone book toward him, he looked expectantly at the older man. "What's his last name?"

"Jacob doesn't have a phone."

Cabe took his frustration out on the phone book by flinging it across the room. It landed on the floor with a loud thump. "Jacob doesn't have a phone. Summer doesn't have a phone. I've never seen so many people who don't have phones. How in the hell do they ever expect people to get a hold of them?"

Richard sipped his drink. "I believe that's why neither one of them has a phone. They don't particularly care whether people can contact them or not." He paused a minute while Cabe paced restlessly. "There's probably some simple explanation for Summer's vanishing act. Maybe she stopped at Celia's and they got to talking and she forgot the time."

"I called. Celia hasn't seen her. This isn't like

Summer, Richard. She's the most responsible person I know. She would have called me if she was going to be late—unless something's happened to her. I'm going crazy just sitting here doing nothing. I don't even have a car to go look for her."

Richard sat his drink aside, then slapped his hands on his knees and stood up. "I'll tell you what. You drive me home and keep the car. Use it as long as you need it. I'll use my wife's car."

"I'll take you up on that, Richard. Thanks. One place I want to check is the island. Do you know where Jacob lives? I want to take a boat out there, and he can let me into the marina to get one." He rubbed the back of his neck. "If she isn't there, I don't know where else to look, but I'll camp out at her cabin if I have to."

"She'll turn up eventually. Women get some strange notions sometimes." Giving Cabe a knowing look, he added, "You'd better get used to it. Summer's one of the most independent women I know. She's been on her own a long time and isn't used to having to notify anyone of her whereabouts."

As Cabe accompanied Richard to his car, he thought about what the older man had said and promised himself a heart-to-heart talk with Summer when he found her. Maybe she didn't have anyone to answer to before, but she was going to have to accept that he had a few rights where she was concerned.

And he would find her.

When Summer walked out of the restaurant, she had a new manager for the marina. Theresa and her husband, Jerry, were enthusiastic about the opportunity she offered them and jumped at the chance to have a bigger income. Jerry got along with Jacob as well as anyone did, so there would be no danger of Jacob disliking the change of management. Neither would taking over immediately pose any problems for the couple. They were eager and willing to do anything Summer wanted them to do.

She hadn't expected to have that part of her plan settled so quickly. Now she was free to go to the airport. After leaving Hadley's house, she had returned briefly to fling on a white wrap-around skirt and a yellow shirt, which were more appropriate to travel in than her shorts and T-shirt. She didn't take the time to pack a suitcase. Whatever else she needed she would buy with the cash she had taken out of the office safe, and she had her credit cards.

A half hour later she held her airline ticket in her hand but two hours to wait until she could use it. Since she had time, she went in search of a pay phone. Celia would be worried about her sudden disappearance if she called and learned Summer was gone.

Celia answered the phone after the first ring. As soon as she heard Summer's voice, she demanded, "Where in the world are you?"

"I'm at the airport. I'm going to be out of town for a couple of days."

"Where are you going?" she asked in bewilderment.

"I'm flying down to Orlando, Florida, but I'll be back by the weekend."

"What about the marina?"

"Theresa and her husband are going to be taking over for me. They'll be managing the marina from now on."

There was a short pause on the other end of the line. Then Celia asked quietly, "What's going on,

Summer? Cabe's been calling me every ten minutes looking for you."

Summer bit her lip. She didn't want to talk about Cabe. "I have a few things to take care of out of town. That's all."

Because she rarely ever went anywhere, she doubted Celia was going to buy her vague reply, but she wasn't ready to tell her the whole story right now. Nor was she ready to answer Celia's next question.

"Have you let Cabe know where you'll be? He sounded frantic when he couldn't find you."

"I'll see him when I get back." There was no way she was going to talk to him now, not until she had something concrete to present to him. "I've got to go, Celia. I'll call you when I get back."

It was obvious Celia wasn't happy about it, but all she said was, "I hope you know what you're doing."

Celia's words echoed her own thoughts. She hoped she knew what she was doing too. She might not be doing the right thing, but she had to at least do something.

Time went by slowly. She would have preferred taking a flight that left immediately but she hadn't been that lucky. Although she hadn't eaten a thing all day, she didn't bother to get any food from the snack bars or the restaurant. She didn't pace the floor or talk to any of the other passengers waiting for the flight. Instead she sat in one of the uncomfortable plastic chairs staring out the window watching the planes land and take off . . . and thinking.

Finally the flight was announced, and she dug her ticket out of the pocket of her skirt. Holding it in her hand, she started toward the gate. She was about to hand it to the attendant, when a hand clamped down on her wrist and the ticket was yanked away.

Even before she turned around, she knew who it was. Cabe pulled her out of the line of other passengers. She protested when he began leading her out of the waiting room.

"Give me back my ticket, Cabe."

"You won't need it," he said coolly. His fingers tightened painfully around her wrist when she tried to wrench away from him. He balled up her ticket and threw it casually into a trash bin as they passed it.

There was no need to ask him how he'd known she was at the airport. The only other person who could have told him was Celia. It didn't matter how he'd found out anyway. He had found her and he was furious.

She practically had to run to keep up with him, but she no longer tried to stop him by attempting to tug her arm free. He was much stronger than she and determined. She did try to halt him with words. "Let me go, Cabe. I'm going to miss my flight."

"Yes," he agreed. "You are."

Instead of turning in the direction of the exit, he walked her down a concourse, past a number of departure and arrival gates, ending up at a familiar waiting room. She started to ask what they were doing there, but he didn't give her a chance. Tugging at her wrist, he forced her to follow him through the same gate she had raced through the day he had arrived on a chartered plane.

An executive jet similar to the one he had arrived in was waiting on the tarmac, the engine on the far side roaring. Cabe shifted his hands to her waist and almost lifted her up the steps into the interior of the plane.

There were no rows of seats as in a regular plane. Instead there were two chairs facing the rear and two other chairs facing them with tables in between. In the back of the plane were two curved sofas, and this is where Cabe took her.

He pressed her down onto one of the sofas and ordered, "Stay there."

A man wearing a uniform was closing the hatch. Cabe spoke to him for a few seconds. The man nodded and walked forward into the cockpit. Summer could see the pilot was already seated there, and heard the other engine start.

Cabe came back and sat down next to her. "Fasten your seat belt. We're going to be taking off."

She was frozen. She couldn't believe this was happening.

After he had his own belt in place, he reached over and snapped hers for her. "Sit back and relax. We'll be in the air a little more than an hour."

The plane was moving now, and there was no way Summer could stop it. "Why are you doing this, Cabe?" she asked quietly.

He considered her question for a moment. "There seem to be a few things we need to iron out and you can't run away from me while we're in the air."

"I wasn't running away," she said defensively. "I was going to Orlando to talk to Fausto. I was coming back."

"I'm pleased to hear it and I hate to get picky, but I can't help but be curious why you were going in the first place without mentioning it to me."

He was being mildly sarcastic, but she could hear the underlying bitterness. "I wasn't going anywhere until I stopped by Hadley's around three and heard you talking to Reese on the phone about selling off the carousel." She ignored his surprised intake of breath and continued. "I was going to see Fausto to ask him if he had any ideas how I could save the horses."

"So that's what this is all about," he muttered. Since they had safely taken off, he unfastened his seat belt and turned sideways to face her. He didn't touch her, though. "If you had stuck around, you would have heard why I was discussing the carousel in the first place. I wasn't making arrangements to sell it, Summer. I was trying to find out its value so that it could be insured."

"Insured?"

"We can't have children riding on the horses without some form of insurance. It's not good business."

Her mouth dropped open in astonishment. "What children? What business?"

"I was planing on discussing this over a candlelight dinner at Hadley's tonight, but it seems the guest of honor decided to leave town." Anger still simmered in his dark eyes as he looked down at her. "I was going to suggest we open the amusement park again, but I wanted to get the facts and figures straight before I presented the idea to you."

Summer slumped against the back of the sofa. Closing her eyes as shame washed over her, she realized too late how wrong she had been about him. "I didn't know," she murmured. She opened her eyes and turned her head to look at him. "I'm sorry, Cabe. I didn't know what you were doing."

"If you had stayed and confronted me with your suspicions, I could have cleared everything up. We could have sat down and discussed it. But no, you had to go off half-cocked to save your precious carousel." His earlier fury came storming back. "How could you think I could do something like that? I thought you knew me better than that by now."

"I thought I did too. That's why it hurt to think you could sell the carousel when you knew how much it meant to me."

His hands framed her face. "What exactly does love mean to you, Summer? To me, it isn't only making love but living love. I can't imagine living without you or your love. It means I trust you with my love. You're going to have to learn to trust me with yours. I would never do anything to hurt you. Not while there is breath left in me."

Tears welled up in her eyes. She lowered her lashes, looking down at her hands clenched in her lap. "I find it hard to believe you do love me, I suppose."

The pressure of his fingers forced her to raise her eyes to his. "I guess I'll have to convince you, then." He lowered his head and caught a tear with his tongue. "If it takes the rest of our lives, I'll do my damndest to show you you're my life, my love."

She twined her arms around his neck and pressed herself against him, burying her face into his neck. Her eyes closed as his arms embraced her. What a fool she'd been. "When a dream comes true," she said, her voice muffled and tremulous, "it's hard to accept it as real."

"This is real, very real. Before I came back to Clearview, I felt something was missing, something vital, something I couldn't pin down. I just knew it wasn't there. Then I met you, and you filled that emptiness." He drew back so that he could see her face. "I do love you, Summer."

"I love you, Cabe," she whispered.

He shuddered in her arms as the words he needed to hear flowed through him, cleansing his spirit and drowning out all his doubts. "Oh, God, Summer. Don't ever leave me like that again."

This time when he kissed her, there was love and tenderness mixed with a shattering passion that had been intensified by their brief misunderstanding. When he raised his head, he murmured, "If we keep this up, we're going to shock our pilot."

"At the moment, I don't care." Her eyes reflected her own desire.

He smiled. "It can wait until we land."

"Land where?"

He loosened his arms around her and took her hands in his. "We're going to Chicago long enough to gather up Reese and his wife and some clothes, and then we're catching a flight to Hawaii."

She gaped at him, her shock genuine. "We're . . . we're . . ." She swallowed with difficulty. "Why?"

Amusement flickered in his eyes. "We need witnesses."

"For what?"

He shook his head in mock censure. "Summer, I have always thought you were an intelligent woman. Surely you can figure it out." She continued to look at him blankly. "We're going to be married in Hawaii, and since neither of us has any family, I thought it would be nice if some friends could share the day with us."

"How did you get all this arranged so quickly?"

Holding her securely in his arms, he leaned back against the sofa, bringing her with him. "After you called Celia, she got on the phone and finally chased me down at the marina, where I had gone looking for you. I called Reese, and he arranged for the charter plane while I headed for the airport. I'm going to tie you to me with as many bonds as I can."

She arched her head back so that she could see his face. "Dreams really do come true. You may have to pinch me once in a while to convince me this is all real."

His smile was blatantly sensual. "I'll find a way to convince you that is much better than pinching you." Lowering his head, he touched her lips lightly, not daring to kiss her the way he wanted to, considering where they were. "This isn't a dream, Tinkerbell. This is fate. You're my fate." He kissed her again and murmured against her mouth, "My love. My life." Then after running his tongue over her bottom lip, he added, "And soon my wife."

As his mouth closed over hers, Summer finally believed all her dreams had indeed come true. She had caught the brass ring after all.

Epilogue

The carousel horses proudly pranced up and down as children and a few adults rode on their backs. The music swelled, and the hundreds of lights shone brilliantly over the laughing children and their smiling parents.

This was the second season the amusement park had been open to the public, and it was a rousing success with the tourists and the local citizens of Clearview. The city council had graciously allowed the necessary permits after Cabe had donated a large piece of Hadley's property to the city to be used as a park.

He had kept the house for their use when they came back to Clearview for the summer months. Occasionally he would have to fly back to Chicago during their stay at the lake, but his work schedule was lighter for those three months so that he could spend time with his family.

Because of his new responsibilities, Cabe had accepted a promotion that gave him the chance to use his experience and knowledge without getting physically involved in undercover work.

Fausto had helped him find an experienced manager for the amusement park, and Theresa and Jerry were still in charge of the marina. Summer had offered them the chance to buy it, but they were content with managing the facilities, leaving the final major decisions up to Cabe and Summer.

Standing on the platform on one side of a white, gaily decorated horse, Cabe smiled at his wife standing on the other side. Both of them were holding on to the laughing toddler, whose little hands grasped the brass pole.

"She's definitely her mother's daughter," he said.

Summer smiled at the joy on little Samantha's face. "I was beginning to wonder if she would ever like the ride. Last time we put her on the carousel, she cried until we took her off."

"Summer, she was six months old."

"Well, she loves it now. Next year we won't be able to keep her off it." She looked over the back of the horse at her husband. "Next year she'll have company."

It took a moment for Cabe to realize what she was saying. Then he lifted his daughter off the horse and walked around it to Summer. "Are you sure?"

She nodded. "I haven't been to the doctor, but I'm sure."

He leaned over and kissed her, then grinned. "Maybe I'd better design a new ride for the park called Flynn's Fate and keep adding more seats as we go along."

She smiled. "Let's keep it to a ride for three or four. Okay?"

His free arm encircled her waist. "'Darling, if it's fate, there isn't anything we can do about it. I've accepted mine."

THE EDITOR'S CORNER

What a wonderful summer of romance reading we have in store for you. Truly, you're going to be LOVESWEPT with some happy surprises through the long, hot, lazy days ahead.

First, you're going to get **POCKETS FULL OF JOY,** LOVESWEPT #270, by our new Canadian author, Judy Gill. Elaina McIvor wondered helplessly what she was going to do with an eleven-month-old baby to care for. Dr. "Brad" Bradshaw had been the stork and deposited the infant on her doorstep and raced away. But he was back soon enough to "play doctor" and "play house" in one of the most delightful and sensuous romances of the season.

Joan Elliott Pickart has created two of her most intriguing characters ever in **TATTERED WINGS,** LOVESWEPT #271. Devastatingly handsome Mark Hampton—an Air Force Colonel whose once exciting life now seems terribly lonely—and beautiful, enigmatic Eden Landry—a top fashion model who left her glamorous life for a secluded ranch— meet one snowy night. Desire flares immediately. But so do problems. Mark soon discovers that Eden is like a perfect butterfly encased in a cube of glass. You'll revel in the ways he finds to break down the walls without hurting the woman!

For all of you who've written to ask for Tara's and Jed's love story, here your fervent requests

(continued)

are answered with Barbara Boswell's terrific **AND TARA, TOO,** LOVESWEPT #272. As we know, Jed Ramsey is as darkly sleek and as seductive and as winning with women as a man can be. And Tara Brady wants no part of him. It would be just too convenient, she thinks, if all the Brady sisters married Ramsey men. But that's exactly what Jed's tyrannical father has in mind. You'll chuckle and gasp as Tara and Jed rattle the chains of fate in a breathlessly sensual and touching love story.

Margie McDonnell is an author who can transport you to another world. This time she takes you to **THE LAND OF ENCHANTMENT,** via LOVESWEPT #273, to meet a modern-day, ever so gallant knight, dashing Patrick Knight, and the sensitive and lovely Karen Harris. Karen is the single parent of an exceptional son and a quite sensible lady . . . until she falls for the handsome hunk who is as merry as he is creative. We think you'll delight in this very special, very thrilling love story.

It gives us enormous pleasure next month to celebrate the fifth anniversary of Iris Johansen's writing career. Her first ever published book was LOVESWEPT's **STORMY VOWS** in August 1983. With that and its companion romance **TEMPEST AT SEA,** published in September 1983, Iris launched the romance featuring spin-off and/or continuing characters. Now everyone's doing it! But, still,

(continued)

nobody does it quite like the woman who began it all, Iris Johansen. Here, next month, you'll meet old friends and new lovers in **BLUE SKIES AND SHINING PROMISES,** LOVESWEPT #274. (The following month she'll also have a LOVESWEPT, of course, and we wonder if you can guess who the featured characters will be.) Don't miss the thrilling love story of Cameron Bandor (yes, you know him) and Damita Shaughnessy, whose background will shock, surprise and move you, taking you right back to five years ago!

Welcome, back, Peggy Webb! In the utterly bewitching LOVESWEPT #275, **SLEEPLESS NIGHTS,** Peggy tells the story of Tanner Donovan of the quicksilver eyes and Amanda Lassiter of the tart tongue and tender heart. In this thrilling and sensuous story, you have a marvelous battle of wits between lovers parted in the past and determined to best each other in the present. A real delight!

As always, we hope that not one of our LOVE-SWEPTs will ever disappoint you. Enjoy!

Carolyn Nichols

Carolyn Nichols
  Editor
LOVESWEPT
Bantam Books
666 Fifth Avenue
New York, NY 10103

THE HOMETOWN HUNK CONTEST

FOR EVERY WOMAN WHO HAS EVER SAID—
"I know a man who looks
just like the hero of this book".
—HAVE WE GOT A CONTEST FOR YOU!

To help celebrate our fifth year of publishing LOVESWEPT we are having a fabulous, fun-filled event called THE HOMETOWN HUNK contest. We are going to reissue six classic early titles by six of your favorite authors.

> *DARLING OBSTACLES* by Barbara Boswell
> *IN A CLASS BY ITSELF* by Sandra Brown
> *C.J.'S FATE* by Kay Hooper
> *THE LADY AND THE UNICORN* by Iris Johansen
> *CHARADE* by Joan Elliott Pickart
> *FOR THE LOVE OF SAMI* by Fayrene Preston

Here, as in the backs of all July, August, and September 1988 LOVESWEPTS you will find "cover notes" just like the ones we prepare at Bantam as the background for our art director to create our covers. These notes will describe the hero and heroine, give a teaser on the plot, and suggest a scene for the cover. Your part in the contest will be to see if a great looking local man—or men, if your hometown is so blessed—fits our description of one of the heroes of the six books we will reissue.

THE HOMETOWN HUNK who is selected (one for each of the six titles) will be flown to New York via United Airlines and will stay at the Loews Summit Hotel—the ideal hotel for business or pleasure in midtown Manhattan—for two nights. All travel arrangements made by Reliable Travel International, Incorporated. He will be the model for the new cover of the book which will be released in mid-1989. The six people who send in the winning photos of their HOMETOWN HUNK will receive a pre-selected assortment of LOVESWEPT books free for one year. Please see the Official Rules above the Official Entry Form for full details and restrictions.

We can't wait to start judging those pictures! Oh, and you must let the man you've chosen know that you're entering him in the contest. After all, if he wins he'll have to come to New York.

Have fun. Here's your chance to get the cover-lover of your dreams!

Carolyn Nichols

Carolyn Nichols
Editor
LOVESWEPT
Bantam Books
666 Fifth Avenue
New York, NY 10102—0023

THE HOMETOWN HUNK CONTEST

DARLING OBSTACLES
(Originally Published as LOVESWEPT #95)
By Barbara Boswell

COVER NOTES

The Characters:

Hero:
GREG WILDER's gorgeous body and "to-die-for" good looks haven't hurt him in the dating department, but when most women discover he's a widower with four kids, they head for the hills! Greg has the hard, muscular build of an athlete, and his light brown hair, which he wears neatly parted on the side, is streaked blond by the sun. Add to that his aquamarine blue eyes that sparkle when he laughs, and his sensual mouth and generous lower lip, and you're probably wondering what woman in her right mind wouldn't want Greg's strong, capable surgeon's hands working their magic on her—kids or no kids!

Personality Traits:
An acclaimed neurosurgeon, Greg Wilder is a celebrity of sorts in the planned community of Woodland, Maryland. Authoritative, debonair, self-confident, his reputation for engaging in one casual relationship after another almost overshadows his prowess as a doctor. In reality, Greg dates more out of necessity than anything else, since he has to attend one social function after another. He considers most of the events boring and wishes he could spend more time with his children. But his profession is a difficult and demanding one—and being both father and mother to four kids isn't any less so. A thoughtful, generous, sometimes befuddled father, Greg tries to do it all. Cerebral, he uses his intellect and skill rather than physical strength to win his victories. However, he never expected to come up against one Mary Magdalene May!

Heroine:
MARY MAGDALENE MAY, called Maggie by her friends, is the thirty-two-year-old mother of three children. She has shoulder-length auburn hair, and green eyes that shout her Irish heritage. With high cheekbones and an upturned nose covered with a smattering of freckles, Maggie thinks of herself more as the girl-next-door type. Certainly, she believes, she could never be one of Greg Wilder's beautiful escorts.

Setting: The small town of Woodland, Maryland

The Story:
Surgeon Greg Wilder wanted to court the feisty and beautiful widow who'd been caring for his four kids, but she just wouldn't let him past her doorstep! Sure that his interest was only casual, and that he preferred more sophisticated women, Maggie May vowed to keep Greg at arm's length. But he wouldn't take no for an answer. And once he'd crashed through her defenses and pulled her into his arms, he was tireless—and reckless—in his campaign to win her over. Maggie had found it tough enough to resist one determined doctor; now he threatened to call in his kids and hers as reinforcements—seven rowdy snags to romance!

Cover scene:
As if romancing Maggie weren't hard enough, Greg can't seem to find time to spend with her without their children around. Stealing a private moment on the stairs in Maggie's house, Greg and Maggie embrace. She is standing one step above him, but she still has to look up at him to see into his eyes. Greg's hands are on her hips, and her hands are resting on his shoulders. Maggie is wearing a very sheer, short pink nightgown, and Greg has on wheat-colored jeans and a navy and yellow striped rugby shirt. Do they have time to kiss?

THE HOMETOWN HUNK CONTEST

IN A CLASS BY ITSELF
(Originally Published as LOVESWEPT #66)
By Sandra Brown

COVER NOTES

The Characters:

Hero:
LOGAN WEBSTER would have no trouble posing for a
Scandinavian travel poster. His wheat-colored hair always
seems to be tousled, defying attempts to control it, and
falls across his wide forehead. Thick eyebrows one shade
darker than his hair accentuate his crystal blue eyes. He
has a slender nose that flairs slightly over a mouth that
testifies to both sensitivity and strength. The faint lines
around his eyes and alongside his mouth give the impression that reaching the ripe age of 30 wasn't all fun and
games for him. Logan's square, determined jaw is punctu-
ated by a vertical cleft. His broad shoulders and narrow
waist add to his tall, lean appearance.

Personality traits:
Logan Webster has had to scrape and save and fight for
everything he's gotten. Born into a poor farm family, he
was driven to succeed and overcome his "wrong side of
the tracks" image. His businesses include cattle, real estate, and natural gas. Now a pillar of the community,
Logan's life has been a true rags-to-riches story. Only
Sandra Brown's own words can describe why he is masculinity epitomized: "Logan had 'the walk,' that saddle-
tramp saunter that was inherent to native Texan men,
passed down through generations of cowboys. It was, without even trying to be, sexy. The unconscious roll of the
hips, the slow strut, the flexed knees, the slouching stance,
the deceptive laziness that hid a latent aggressiveness."
Wow! And not only does he have "the walk," but he's fun

and generous and kind. Even with his wealth, he feels at home living in his small hometown with simple, hard-working, middle-class, backbone-of-America folks. A born leader, people automatically gravitate toward him.

Heroine:

DANI QUINN is a sophisticated twenty-eight-year-old woman. Dainty, her body compact, she is utterly feminine. Dani's pale, lustrous hair is moonlight and honey spun together, and because it is very straight, she usually wears it in a chignon. With golden eyes to match her golden hair, Dani is the one woman Logan hasn't been able to get off his mind for the ten years they've been apart.

Setting: Primarily on Logan's ranch in East Texas.

The Story:

Ten years had passed since Dani Quinn had graduated from high school in the small Texas town, ten years since the night her elopement with Logan Webster had ended in disaster. Now Dani approached her tenth reunion with uncertainty. Logan would be there . . . Logan, the only man who'd ever made her shiver with desire and need, but would she have the courage to face the fury in his eyes? She couldn't defend herself against his anger and hurt—to do so would demand she reveal the secret sorrow she shared with no one. Logan's touch had made her his so long ago. Could he reach past the pain to make her his for all time?

Cover Scene:

It's sunset, and Logan and Dani are standing beside the swimming pool on his ranch, embracing. The pool is surrounded by semitropical plants and lush flower beds. In the distance, acres of rolling pasture land resembling a green lake undulate into dense, piney woods. Dani is wearing a strapless, peacock blue bikini and sandals with leather ties that wrap around her ankles. Her hair is straight and loose, falling to the middle of her back. Logan has on a light-colored pair of corduroy shorts and a short-sleeved designer knit shirt in a pale shade of yellow.

THE HOMETOWN HUNK CONTEST

C.J.'S FATE
(Originally Published as LOVESWEPT #32)
By Kay Hooper

COVER NOTES

The Characters:

Hero:
FATE WESTON easily could have walked straight off an Indian reservation. His raven black hair and strong, well-molded features testify to his heritage. But somewhere along the line genetics threw Fate a curve—his eyes are the deepest, darkest blue imaginable! Above those blue eyes are dark slanted eyebrows, and fanning out from those eyes are faint laugh lines—the only sign of the fact that he's thirty-four years old. Tall, Fate moves with easy, loose-limbed grace. Although he isn't an athlete, Fate takes very good care of himself, and it shows in his strong physique. Striking at first glance and fascinating with each succeeding glance, the serious expressions on his face make him look older than his years, but with one smile he looks boyish again.

Personality traits:
Fate possesses a keen sense of humor. His heavy-lidded, intelligent eyes are capable of concealment, but there is a shrewdness in them that reveals the man hadn't needed college or a law degree to be considered intelligent. The set of his head tells you that he is proud—perhaps even a bit arrogant. He is attractive and perfectly well aware of that fact. Unconventional, paradoxical, tender, silly, lusty, gentle, comical, serious, absurd, and endearing are all words that come to mind when you think of Fate. He is not ashamed to be everything a man can be. A defense attorney by profession, one can detect a bit of frustrated actor in his character. More than anything else, though, it's the

impression of humor about him—reinforced by the elusive dimple in his cheek—that makes Fate Weston a scrumptious hero!

Heroine:
C.J. ADAMS is a twenty-six-year-old research librarian. Unaware of her own attractiveness, C.J. tends to play down her pixylike figure and tawny gold eyes. But once she meets Fate, she no longer feels that her short, burnished copper curls and the sprinkling of freckles on her nose make her unappealing. He brings out the vixen in her, and changes the smart, bookish woman who professed to have no interest in men into the beautiful, sexy woman she really was all along. Now, if only he could get her to tell him what C.J. stands for!

Setting: Ski lodge in Aspen, Colorado

The Story:
C.J. Adams had been teased enough about her seeming lack of interest in the opposite sex. On a ski trip with her five best friends, she impulsively embraced a handsome stranger, pretending they were secret lovers—and the delighted lawyer who joined in her impetuous charade seized the moment to deepen the kiss. Astonished at his reaction, C.J. tried to nip their romance in the bud—but found herself nipping at his neck instead! She had met her match in a man who could answer her witty remarks with clever ripostes of his own, and a lover whose caresses aroused in her a passionate need she'd never suspected that she could feel. Had destiny somehow tossed them together?

Cover Scene:
C.J. and Fate virtually have the ski slopes to themselves early one morning, and they take advantage of it! Frolicking in a snow drift, Fate is covering C.J. with snow—and kisses! They are flushed from the cold weather and from the excitement of being in love. C.J. is wearing a sky-blue, one-piece, tight-fitting ski outfit that zips down the front. Fate is wearing a navy blue parka and matching ski pants.

THE HOMETOWN HUNK CONTEST

THE LADY AND THE UNICORN
(Originally Published as LOVESWEPT #29)
By Iris Johansen

COVER NOTES

The Characters:

Hero:
Not classically handsome, RAFE SANTINE's blunt, craggy features reinforce the quality of overpowering virility about him. He has wide, Slavic cheekbones and a bold, thrusting chin, which give the impression of strength and authority. Thick black eyebrows are set over piercing dark eyes. He wears his heavy, dark hair long. His large frame measures in at almost six feet four inches, and it's hard to believe that a man with such brawny shoulders and strong thighs could exhibit the pantherlike grace which characterizes Rafe's movements. Rafe Santine is definitely a man to be reckoned with, and heroine Janna Cannon does just that!

Personality traits:
Our hero is a man who radiates an aura of power and danger, and women find him intriguing and irresistible. Rafe Santine is a self-made billionaire at the age of thirty-eight. Almost entirely self-educated, he left school at sixteen to work on his first construction job, and by the time he was twenty-three, he owned the company. From there he branched out into real estate, computers, and oil. Rafe reportedly changes mistresses as often as he changes shirts. His reputation for ruthless brilliance has been earned over years of fighting to the top of the economic ladder from the slums of New York. His gruff manner and hard personality hide the tender, vulnerable side of him. Rafe also possesses an insatiable thirst for knowledge that is a passion with him. Oddly enough, he has a wry sense of

humor that surfaces unexpectedly from time to time. And, though cynical to the extreme, he never lets his natural skepticism interfere with his innate sense of justice.

Heroine:

JANNA CANNON, a game warden for a small wildlife preserve, is a very dedicated lady. She is tall at five feet nine inches and carries herself in a stately way. Her long hair is dark brown and is usually twisted into a single thick braid in back. Of course, Rafe never lets her keep her hair braided when they make love! Janna is one quarter Cherokee Indian by heritage, and she possesses the dark eyes and skin of her ancestors.

Setting: Rafe's estate in Carmel, California

The Story:

Janna Cannon scaled the high walls of Rafe Santine's private estate, afraid of nothing and determined to appeal to the powerful man who could save her beloved animal preserve. She bewitched his guard dogs, then cast a spell of enchantment over him as well. Janna's profound grace, her caring nature, made the tough and proud Rafe grow mercurial in her presence. She offered him a gift he'd never risked reaching out for before—but could he trust his own emotions enough to open himself to her love?

Cover Scene:

In the gazebo overlooking the rugged cliffs at the edge of the Pacific Ocean, Rafe and Janna share a passionate moment together. The gazebo is made of redwood and the interior is small and cozy. Scarlet cushions cover the benches, and matching scarlet curtains hang from the eaves, caught back by tasseled sashes to permit the sea breeze to whip through the enclosure. Rafe is wearing black suede pants and a charcoal gray crew-neck sweater. Janna is wearing a safari-style khaki shirt-and-slacks outfit and suede desert boots. They embrace against the breathtaking backdrop of wild, crashing, white-crested waves pounding the rocks and cliffs below.

THE HOMETOWN HUNK CONTEST

CHARADE
(Originally Published as LOVESWEPT #74)
By Joan Elliott Pickart

COVER NOTES

The Characters:

Hero:
The phrase tall, dark, and handsome was coined to describe TENNES WHITNEY. His coal black hair reaches past his collar in back, and his fathomless steel gray eyes are framed by the kind of thick, dark lashes that a woman would kill to have. Darkly tanned, Tennes has a straight nose and a square chin, with—you guessed it!—a Kirk Douglas cleft. Tennes oozes masculinity and virility. He's a handsome son-of-a-gun!

Personality traits:
A shrewd, ruthless business tycoon, Tennes is a man of strength and principle. He's perfected the art of buying floundering companies and turning them around financially, then selling them at a profit. He possesses a sixth sense about business—in short, he's a winner! But there are two sides to his personality. Always in cool command, Tennes, who fears no man or challenge, is rendered emotionally vulnerable when faced with his elderly aunt's illness. His deep devotion to the woman who raised him clearly casts him as a warm, compassionate guy—not at all like the tough-as-nails executive image he presents. Leave it to heroine Whitney Jordan to discover the real man behind the complicated enigma.

Heroine:
WHITNEY JORDAN's russet-colored hair floats past her shoulders in glorious waves. Her emerald green eyes, full breasts, and long, slender legs—not to mention her peaches-

and-cream complexion—make her eye-poppingly attractive. How can Tennes resist the twenty-six-year-old beauty? And how can Whitney consider becoming serious with him? If their romance flourishes, she may end up being Whitney Whitney!

Setting: Los Angeles, California

The Story:
One moment writer Whitney Jordan was strolling the aisles of McNeil's Department Store, plotting the untimely demise of a soap opera heartthrob; the next, she was nearly knocked over by a real-life stunner who implored her to be his fiancée! The ailing little gray-haired aunt who'd raised him had one final wish, he said—to see her dear nephew Tennes married to the wonderful girl he'd described in his letters . . . only that girl hadn't existed—until now! Tennes promised the masquerade would last only through lunch, but Whitney gave such an inspired performance that Aunt Olive refused to let her go. And what began as a playful romantic deception grew more breathlessly real by the minute. . . .

Cover Scene:
Whitney's living room is bright and cheerful. The gray carpeting and blue sofa with green and blue throw pillows gives the apartment a cool but welcoming appearance. Sitting on the sofa next to Tennes, Whitney is wearing a black crepe dress that is simply cut but stunning. It is cut low over her breasts and held at the shoulders by thin straps. The skirt falls to her knees in soft folds and the bodice is nipped in at the waist with a matching belt. She has on black high heels, but prefers not to wear any jewelry to spoil the simplicity of the dress. Tennes is dressed in a black suit with a white silk shirt and a deep red tie.

THE HOMETOWN HUNK CONTEST

FOR THE LOVE OF SAMI
(Originally Published as LOVESWEPT #34)
By Fayrene Preston

COVER NOTES

Hero:
DANIEL PARKER-ST. JAMES is every woman's dream come true. With glossy black hair and warm, reassuring blue eyes, he makes our heroine melt with just a glance. Daniel's lean face is chiseled into assertive planes. His lips are full and firmly sculptured, and his chin has the determined and arrogant thrust to it only a man who's sure of himself can carry off. Daniel has a lot in common with Clark Kent. Both wear glasses, and when Daniel removes them to make love to Sami, she thinks he really is Superman!

Personality traits:
Daniel Parker-St. James is one of the Twin Cities' most respected attorneys. He's always in the news, either in the society columns with his latest society lady, or on the front page with his headline cases. He's brilliant and takes on only the toughest cases—usually those that involve millions of dollars. Daniel has a reputation for being a deadly opponent in the courtroom. Because he's from a socially prominent family and is a Harvard graduate, it's expected that he'll run for the Senate one day. Distinguished-looking and always distinctively dressed—he's fastidious about his appearance—Daniel gives off an unassailable air of authority and absolute control.

Heroine:
SAMUELINA (SAMI) ADKINSON is secretly a wealthy heiress. No one would guess. She lives in a converted warehouse loft, dresses to suit no one but herself, and dabbles in the creative arts. Sami is twenty-six years old, with

long, honey-colored hair. She wears soft, wispy bangs and has very thick brown lashes framing her golden eyes. Of medium height, Sami has to look up to gaze into Daniel's deep blue eyes.

Setting: St. Paul, Minnesota

The Story:
Unpredictable heiress Sami Adkinson had endeared herself to the most surprising people—from the bag ladies in the park she protected . . . to the mobster who appointed himself her guardian . . . to her exasperated but loving friends. Then Sami was arrested while demonstrating to save baby seals, and it took powerful attorney Daniel Parker-St. James to bail her out. Daniel was smitten, soon cherishing Sami and protecting her from her night fears. Sami reveled in his love—and resisted it too. And holding on to Sami, Daniel discovered, was like trying to hug quicksilver. . . .

Cover Scene:
The interior of Daniel's house is very grand and supremely formal, the decor sophisticated, refined, and quietly tasteful, just like Daniel himself. Rich traditional fabrics cover plush oversized custom sofas and Regency wing chairs. Queen Anne furniture is mixed with Chippendale and is subtly complemented with Oriental accent pieces. In the library, floor-to-ceiling bookcases filled with rare books provide the backdrop for Sami and Daniel's embrace. Sami is wearing a gold satin sheath gown. The dress has a high neckline, but in back is cut provocatively to the waist. Her jewels are exquisite. The necklace is made up of clusters of flowers created by large, flawless diamonds. From every cluster a huge, perfectly matched teardrop emerald hangs. The earrings are composed of an even larger flower cluster, and an equally huge teardrop-shaped emerald hangs from each one. Daniel is wearing a classic, elegant tuxedo.

LOVESWEPT® HOMETOWN HUNK CONTEST

OFFICIAL RULES

IN A CLASS BY ITSELF by Sandra Brown
FOR THE LOVE OF SAMI by Fayrene Preston
C.J.'S FATE by Kay Hooper
THE LADY AND THE UNICORN by Iris Johansen
CHARADE by Joan Elliott Pickart
DARLING OBSTACLES by Barbara Boswell

1. NO PURCHASE NECESSARY. Enter the HOMETOWN HUNK contest by completing the Official Entry Form below and enclosing a sharp color full-length photograph (easy to see details, with the photo being no smaller than 2½" × 3½") of the man you think perfectly represents one of the heroes from the above-listed books which are described in the accompanying Loveswept cover notes. Please be sure to fill out the Official Entry Form completely, and also be sure to clearly print on the back of the man's photograph the man's name, address, city, state, zip code, telephone number, date of birth, your name, address, city, state, zip code, telephone number, your relationship, if any, to the man (e.g. wife, girlfriend) as well as the title of the Loveswept book for which you are entering the man. If you do not have an Official Entry Form, you can print all of the required information on a 3" × 5" card and attach it to the photograph with all the necessary information printed on the back of the photograph as well. YOUR HERO MUST SIGN BOTH THE BACK OF THE OFFICIAL ENTRY FORM (OR 3" × 5" CARD) AND THE PHOTOGRAPH TO SIGNIFY HIS CONSENT TO BEING ENTERED IN THE CONTEST. Completed entries should be sent to:

BANTAM BOOKS
HOMETOWN HUNK CONTEST
Department CN
666 Fifth Avenue
New York, New York 10102–0023

All photographs and entries become the property of Bantam Books and will not be returned under any circumstances.

2. Six men will be chosen by the Loveswept authors as a HOMETOWN HUNK (one HUNK per Loveswept title). By entering the contest, each winner and each person who enters a winner agrees to abide by Bantam Books' rules and to be subject to Bantam Books' eligibility requirements. Each winning HUNK and each person who enters a winner will be required to sign all papers deemed necessary by Bantam Books before receiving any prize. Each winning HUNK will be flown via **United Airlines** from his closest United Airlines-serviced city to New York City and will stay at the ▪▪▪ S**t∵∵**t Hotel—the ideal hotel for business or pleasure in midtown Manhattan— for two nights. Winning HUNKS' meals and hotel transfers will be provided by Bantam Books. Travel and hotel arrangements are made by *RELIABLE TRAVEL INTERNATIONAL, INC.* and are subject to availability and to Bantam Books' date requirements. Each winning HUNK will pose with a female model at a photographer's studio for a photograph that will serve as the basis of a Loveswept front cover. Each winning HUNK will receive a $150.00 modeling fee. Each winning HUNK will be required to sign an Affidavit of Eligibility and Model's Release supplied by Bantam Books. (Approximate retail value of HOMETOWN HUNK'S PRIZE: $900.00). The six people who send in a winning HOMETOWN HUNK photograph that is used by Bantam will receive free for one year each, LOVESWEPT romance paperback books published by Bantam during that year. (Approximate retail value: $180.00.) Each person who submits a winning photograph

will also be required to sign an Affidavit of Eligibility and Promotional Release supplied by Bantam Books. All winning HUNKS' (as well as the people who submit the winning photographs) names, addresses, biographical data and likenesses may be used by Bantam Books for publicity and promotional purposes without any additional compensation. There will be no prize substitutions or cash equivalents made.

3. All completed entries must be received by Bantam Books no later than September 15, 1988. Bantam Books is not responsible for lost or misdirected entries. The finalists will be selected by Loveswept editors and the six winning HOMETOWN HUNKS will be selected by the six authors of the participating Loveswept books. Winners will be selected on the basis of how closely the judges believe they reflect the descriptions of the books' heroes. Winners will be notified on or about October 31, 1988. If there are insufficient entries or if in the judges' opinions, no entry is suitable or adequately reflects the descriptions of the hero(s) in the book(s), Bantam may decide not to award a prize for the applicable book(s) and may reissue the book(s) at its discretion.

4. The contest is open to residents of the U.S. and Canada, except the Province of Quebec, and is void where prohibited by law. All federal and local regulations apply. Employees of Reliable Travel International, Inc., United Airlines, the Summit Hotel, and the Bantam Doubleday Dell Publishing Group, Inc., their subsidiaries and affiliates, and their immediate families are ineligible to enter.

5. For an extra copy of the Official Rules, the Official Entry Form, and the accompanying Loveswept cover notes, send your request and a self-addressed stamped envelope (Vermont and Washington State residents need not affix postage) before August 20, 1988 to the address listed in Paragraph 1 above.

LOVESWEPT® HOMETOWN HUNK OFFICIAL ENTRY FORM

BANTAM BOOKS
HOMETOWN HUNK CONTEST
Dept. CN
666 Fifth Avenue
New York, New York 10102–0023

HOMETOWN HUNK CONTEST

YOUR NAME_____

YOUR ADDRESS_____

CITY_____ STATE_____ ZIP_____

THE NAME OF THE LOVESWEPT BOOK FOR WHICH YOU ARE ENTERING THIS PHOTO

_____by_____

YOUR RELATIONSHIP TO YOUR HERO_____

YOUR HERO'S NAME_____

YOUR HERO'S ADDRESS_____

CITY_____ STATE_____ ZIP_____

YOUR HERO'S TELEPHONE #_____

YOUR HERO'S DATE OF BIRTH_____

YOUR HERO'S SIGNATURE CONSENTING TO HIS PHOTOGRAPH ENTRY

_____

THE DELANEY DYNASTY

Men and women whose loves and passions are so glorious it takes many great romance novels by three bestselling authors to tell their tempestuous stories.

THE SHAMROCK TRINITY

- ☐ 21786 RAFE, THE MAVERICK
  by Kay Hooper $2.75
- ☐ 21787 YORK, THE RENEGADE
  by Iris Johansen $2.75
- ☐ 21788 BURKE, THE KINGPIN
  by Fayrene Preston $2.75

THE DELANEYS OF KILLAROO

- ☐ 21872 ADELAIDE, THE ENCHANTRESS
  by Kay Hooper $2.75
- ☐ 21873 MATILDA, THE ADVENTURESS
  by Iris Johansen $2.75
- ☐ 21874 SYDNEY, THE TEMPTRESS
  by Fayrene Preston $2.75

- ☐ 26991 THIS FIERCE SPLENDOR
  by Iris Johansen $3.95

Now Available!

THE DELANEYS: *The Untamed Years*

- ☐ 21897 GOLDEN FLAMES *by Kay Hooper* $3.50
- ☐ 21898 WILD SILVER *by Iris Johansen* $3.50
- ☐ 21999 COPPER FIRE *by Fayrene Preston* $3.50

Buy these books at your local bookstore or use the handy coupon below.

Prices and availability subject to change without notice.

- -

Bantam Books, Dept. SW7, 414 East Golf Road, Des Plaines, IL 60016

Please send me the books I have checked above. I am enclosing $_____
(please add $2.00 to cover postage and handling). Send check or money order—no cash or C.O.D.s please.

Mr/Ms _____

Address _____

City/State _____ Zip _____

SW7—7/88

Please allow four to six weeks for delivery. This offer expires 1/89.

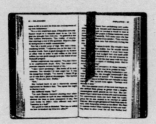